Spooky Tales and Scary Things

Short Stories To Read With The Lights On

HARRY CARPENTER

First edition

ISBN: 978-1090541031

Dedication This is dedicated to my friends, family, and co-workers that thought this was a cool story or was interested in the spooky things I could come up with.

Thanks for the support. Thanks to my wife for going through and proofreading this story and correcting my excessive use of commas, ands, buts, and the other things that annoyed her. But she knows I love her.

Monsters are real, and ghosts are real too. They live inside us, and sometimes, they win. - Stephen King

Contents

1

The General

Leaves fell from trees as fall crept across the East Coast. It was late September in 2004, and the crisp air swept through the row home filled neighborhood in which Freddy resided. He was your average nineteen-year-old, with typical tastes of that age; MTV and rock music, video games, and computer use. You see, Freddy was a warehouse employee in the afternoons. He spent his shifts moving boxes, product and fulfilling orders. Freddy always hated working for someone else. However, at night, he was able to run the show as a late-night radio DJ on an online streaming radio show.

Typically, in Freddy's life, nothing ever went his way. His experience in high school was pretty rough. Always being persecuted by school police, bullying by other students, and a lack of a love life really weighed down on Freddy. He bounced from job to job, never really finding a sense of belonging. DJing changed his whole perspective on life. It gave him creative power and an outlet to be himself.

It was five o'clock in the evening, and it was time to head to work. Freddy wore his typical jeans and video game shirt and walked to work. He didn't own a car but luckily managed to land jobs within a reasonable distance. Freddy put on his Discman CD player and large foam headphones and started out the door. He called out to his mom to let her know he was leaving. After that, he closed the door behind him and left for work.

The walk was anything but eventful. There were a few people on their porches, several children playing in the street, but nothing that was of danger or out of place. Freddy lived in a rough neighborhood where violence was prevalent, but it never seemed to faze him. He stopped at the local gas station, just a block or two from work to retrieve his usual energy drink and sandwich. It was the pre-work meal that gave him the extra boost he needed to survive yet another eight-hour workday. The shop wasn't too far away from the warehouse, so it wasn't much of a detour.

Freddy performed his typical shift work. He filled orders of automotive parts, pulled the parts down from shelving, and loaded them onto the wooden pallets for transport. He worked alone in a warehouse, while the rest of the staff worked in the main building. Being alone didn't bother him because he had the comfort of his music. He burned mix CDs of songs he loved, and that got him through each workday. Even though it was starting to cool down outside, it was very much a heat box inside of the warehouse building.

Lunch break was typically spent alone, sitting outside of the building. It wasn't that Freddy wasn't friends with anyone at work, it was that he was more of a loner and socially awkward. He felt it best to stay out of everyone's way. The warehouse was huge, and it wasn't hard to disappear within the building. It was a maze of aisles and rows of merchandise to prepare for the client's shipping requests. The air was always dusty and felt thick. This and wanting to just be alone were valid reasons for Freddy to post up outside by the vehicles, or so he thought.

One of the senior employees, Jason, approached him.

"Duder, are you hungry? We are going to run to the store and grab something since the computer is down. We have time. You in?" Freddy didn't really look up and gave Jason a passive shrug. "I know you need some caffeine. Some soda therapy?" With that, Freddy looked up and started to his feet.

"I knew that would get you. Come on, we are taking my car."

The two headed toward Jason's car. He owned a nice sporty car, a Pontiac Firebird. It was pretty stylish and cool, so Freddy thought. They buckled in, along with two other guys from the shop, and drove out of the parking lot toward the nearby convenience store.

Getting out and seeing the world during a work shift was a nice touch to break up the day. Freddy wandered the aisles, grabbing a bag of chips and a large bottle of Coke. They piled back up into the car and traveled the path back to work. Jason blared his latest Limp Bizkit album, and Freddy drank a few sips of his soda in the back seat of the car. They pulled back into the parking lot and piled out of the vehicle. Some of the guys were joking and having a good time, but Freddy put his headphones back on and slipped back into his mental zone.

Lunch break was called to an end, and the computers were back online. Orders were being printed, and items were being pulled. Freddy worked pretty hard and wrapped up his work for the day. He headed over to the central warehouse to assist in the packaging and loading of the product into the trucks. This was the only time Freddy became sociable, as communication was vital to do this work. He would use a plastic shrink-wrapping tool to wrap up the product and call out to the forklift operators to take it to the designated truck. Everyone knew that if this part went quickly and efficiently, an early work call was a possibility.

The crew pushed through the work and managed to knock everything out around 11 PM. The guys played football for a bit while the final paperwork was completed. Just around fifteen minutes later, the foreman dismissed everyone. Freddy grabbed his bookbag and belongings from his locker and made his way to the parking lot.

"Hey duder, you want a lift? Save you some time and energy."

It was Jason, walking toward his car. Freddy shrugged and joined him in the car. He was pretty happy to have gotten a ride home since it gave him more time before his real passion: the radio.

The ride home was nice. Freddy had no need to worry about any fights, moving quickly, or looking over his shoulder. The ride was anything but quiet as Jason blared his favorite music as loud as possible. Freddy didn't seem to mind much. The Firebird pulled up to Freddy's row home around eleven-thirty.

"Thanks for the ride, man," Freddy said as he was closing the car door.

Jason peeled out of the neighborhood, and Freddy was alone. Quietly opening the noisy rusted gate to the small yard at the front of his house, he crept into the house and made his way to the basement. It was his comfort place, and it had everything he could possibly need; a mini-fridge, television, futon, and a computer. He popped open a TV Dinner, something with chicken, and fired up the desktop PC while it cooked.

Freddy logged into the software to begin the radio broadcast. It was still very early for his shift, so at this point, all he can do is listen and chat with the other DJs through the messenger. The microwave beeped, and he ate his dinner while relaxing and enjoying the songs being played on the shift prior. Seth had an awesome playlist and always played hits. Freddy, Seth, and Nate were the only DJs to be very vocal on their shifts, trying to make something of what was essentially nothing.

The trio was top-rated, and at times, they combined their shows to entertain the people. A message popped up on screen with the typical jingle of the messenger. Freddy leaned in to get a better look at it from the futon. It was from Seth, and it read:

"Hey, bro, do you want to get up on this, and we can crush the next few hours?"

He wanted to have a co-host for the evening. Freddy obliged and began to prepare his microphone and equipment for the air. They cracked jokes of the usual variety. Freddy was good at vocal impressions and would usually be characters from cartoons he enjoyed during the broadcast.

The combo show rolled right into Freddy's shift. Listeners never seemed to mind, as the late-night guys were always entertaining to listen to. Messages continued to pour in through the messenger, which often

struck up a conversation between the guys. Freddy noticed a blinking message waiting for him from an unknown sender. The sender wasn't already a friend on his list, which indicated a new listener, or at best, a new message buddy. The next music break was coming up, so he held it to himself and decided to check it
with Seth.

Seth's curiosity was burning.

"Dude, what does it say?"

"Do you want me to read it now, or wait until we go back on the air? I'm up for a genuine reaction from the two of us if you want," Freddy proposed.

"It's up to you, dude. That might be better. Actually, let me hit up Nate to see if he wants in on this tonight."

Soon after, a message was sent to the third man of the late-night trio. There was some shuffling over the headphones, and Nate's voice spoke up.

"Duuuuuudes!"

He finished fiddling with his setup and was prepared to be live.

"So, what's the dealio with your message? I'm ready to hear this thing," Nate said.

"Wait until after this song, my man," Freddy assured.

The song ended.

"Woooo boy. While we were jamming out, we got hit by an epic message.
Didn't we, Freddy?" Seth hyped up immediately.

"Yeah, give me a sec. Let me sort this out," Freddy mumbled as clicked the message and agreed to read it, "Ok, here goes. I'll read it as I'm seeing it. Y'all ready?"

The other two verbally acknowledged they were ready, and he assumed the listeners were equally prepared. He cleared his throat dramatically and pretended to shuffle papers for comedic effect.

"The message reads: Hey. I hope you don't get weirded out by this, but I'm dead serious when I say this. I'm super scared, and I don't know who else to tell, or what this even sounds like. I'm being haunted by a demon, and tonight is the night he comes for me. Please respond to me," Freddy read.

"Bro, that is deep! Hit him back about his Devil dude!" Nate joked.

The keyboard was afire with a response to this random fan. A few moments went by, and the gang made as much small talk as they could. Then it happened.

"Someone is typing," appeared on the screen.

There was a response imminent.

"I see the response coming! Are you guys pumped to hear this thing? I am.
This is nuts."

Freddy updated everyone who couldn't actually see the screen as he did.

The second message block was much larger than the first, in much more detail.

"Ok, so, here is the thing. I don't have much time. I can hear his hellhounds outside barking. He is outside my bedroom window, and I last saw him standing in my yard. I'm serious, please listen. He calls himself 'The General,' and he looks like an old-time war general. He came to take my soul, and I need help," Freddy read aloud over the air.

"Sounds like he forgot his meds guys. See how we can help this dude? Smoke a blunt or something, chillax or whatever," jested Nate.

Nothing came back over the messenger for the next few moments.

The radio show continued, and a music block began to play.

"So, what is this guy's deal? Did that general dude get him or something?" Seth asked.

"No clue. I should hit him up. Obviously, he was listening to us."

Freddy leaned forward and typed up a response to the mysterious messenger.

6

"What is it we can do? You good?"

There was still no activity on the messenger. To be honest, the guys were feeling a little worried as well. What if something had happened to this mystery caller?

"You've already helped me. Thank you," displayed across the screen.

"What did that even mean?" thought Freddy.

He read the message back to the team and replied right away.

"How? How did we help you?"

There was an immediate reply from the guy.

"Simple. By talking about The General to someone in detail, I've passed it on to you. I'm sorry, but you were the only thing I could think of. You saved me, but I'm sorry."

The messenger window flashed with the message:

"This user has blocked further communication from you," displayed across the screen.

"What. The. Actual. Hell?" Freddy thought.

The music break was coming to a close, so Freddy filled in Nate and Seth on the latest and greatest news.

It was very unsettling, but at the same time obviously bogus, they thought. The gang wrapped up the radio show on a high note, as Nate got high live on the air, as he typically did. Freddy didn't care because they filmed in their own homes, miles away from each other. After they turned over hosting to the next guy, each logged off almost right away. Freddy thought hard about what the guy said and thought it was hilarious. He started cleaning up his area, winding up cords and gathering up any trash when suddenly from the back of the basement something fell. His heart immediately raced, and his skin felt cold from fear.

Panicked, Freddy reached for any sort of weapon he could think of. Who knew what lie beyond the sliding door to the laundry area? There was a back door, perhaps a burglar? Or possibly it was something far worse. He reached for a can of air freshener and a baseball bat, ready to attack. Slowly, he crept into a fighting stance and made his way back to the dark area in the rear of the basement. Finger on the trigger of the spray, he was prepared to blind and beat whoever was foolish enough to enter his domain, so long as they could be blinded and beaten.

Rounding the corner and starting down the dark hallway towards the next light switch. It felt like what seemed like miles away in the center of the room on a pull chain. Again, something fell to the floor as if disturbed by someone or something. His heart raced. He could feel his heartbeat in his hands as he crept toward the room. He didn't notice anyone standing in the room, far as he could tell, so he rushed forward and reached for the light.

"Reeeaaww!"

The cat let out a screech that caused Freddy to turn several shades of colors.

"Damn you, cat! You scared the hell out of me, asshole."

Freddy picked up the bottle of laundry detergent the cat knocked down and scanned the room for anything else out of place. He laughed to himself as he walked back toward his bedroom, unable to even believe he was this worked up over something so stupid. He shut down his computer, threw his garbage away, and bedded down for the night. He had a hard time falling asleep for a while. He was still keyed up from the previous adventure but ultimately drifted off into sleep to prepare for the next day.

The next afternoon, Freddy felt like garbage. He barely slept and tossed and turned most of the night. He woke up at 2 PM to prepare for work, as he always did. The basement bedroom in which he resided lacked any outward facing windows, so it was pitch dark without the lights on. He turned on his side table lamp, which was shaped like a monkey, and tried to manage energy to start his day. After a hot shower and a bowl of oatmeal, he dressed and headed for the door.

Freddy felt a vibration in his pocket. He was getting a call from his coworker, Jason.

"Hey, calling ya because I'm on the road early. Want a lift? Might rain in a bit."

Freddy was not opposed to such generosity, especially if it was going to rain. He refused to carry an umbrella with him.

"Sure, swing by my house in a few?" he asked.

"Yeah, be there in ten."

Jason hung up the phone. Moments later, Jason pulled up, and Freddy got into the car.

"What's new with you, sir?" Jason asked, trying to make conversation rather than blasting the radio. Freddy was quiet. He sometimes told his coworkers stories from his radio time but seldom disclosed them on a regular basis. "You're going to think this one is full-blown batshit crazy." "Try me. I've seen crazy," Jason belted out confidently. "Ok, well, look. You know how I do the radio thing?" Jason nodded.

"Well, we had this crazy dude last night hit us up. He said he was being haunted by a demon, and it was trying to kill him."

"Wow, what a headcase. So, did it get him or something?" Jason asked, playing along.

"Nah, apparently not. It was a joke. But it spooked me last night for sure," Freddy said, reassuring himself.

"Happens when I watch scary movies. I was no good after watching that one Japanese one with the chick that killed everyone. They kept finding her hair everywhere like in closets, their throats, whatever the filmmaker thought

was creepy. That's pretty cool. You got your own little ghost story."

Jason laughed as he said that, making the turn into the gas station near work to pick up a few energy drinks.

Working in the warehouse that day alone, Freddy was positive he kept hearing things and even seeing shadows in the distance down the aisles. Of course, it was all his mind playing tricks on him, he thought. It had to be because when you think you are scared, chances are you'll get scared. He kept his head down, his music up, and pushed through the shift. Lunch break came, and he joined the rest of the crew. Jason was telling everyone about how Freddy was stalked by a crazy guy online last night. The lunch break was spent dismissing all claims, questions, and jokes that everyone had for the next hour. The guys gave up on the idea once work resumed and kept busy.

Freddy kept busy the next few hours, loading up trucks with the product and finishing as quickly as possible. He did all he could to keep his brain from wandering to other thoughts. In the back of his mind, the idea of whatever that kid said online still bugged him. The foreman announced the work was completed for the day, and everyone was able to relax while the final reports came together. Jason headed over to where Freddy was sitting. He looked up from his headphones and stopped his music.

"Hey brother, you need a lift to the parental's house?" Jason inquired.

"Yeah, if you want. It's no big deal if you can't. Don't feel obligated."

"No sweat. I got you, man. I'll be at the car after we all punch out."

Freddy headed over to the Firebird and waited for Jason to join. He was accompanied by two other co-workers who were apparently getting a lift home as well. They all lived in a reasonably small area near each other, so it wasn't too far out of the way to drive. They all piled into the car with Freddy in the back seat. The car was filled with the chatter of getting beers on the weekend and watching the latest football game on Sunday to see the Ravens play against the Steelers. It was an intense conversation, as one of the guys in the car was the only Steelers fan. Friday didn't come fast enough, because it meant Freddy could stay up pretty late and not have to go to work the next day. It was a party night, which meant sitting alone on the computer and playing games after DJing.

The car dumped Freddy off at his house, and he went inside. The usual routine was followed, making something to eat, checking email, and tuning in to the current DJ, Seth, followed by Nate. He sent a message over telling them last night really sucked, and that dude really got to him. It was quickly dismissed as a stupid gag by a fan, and it was business as usual on the air. The three tagged up to be the triple threat night shift trio and continued to amuse everyone through the night. Each two-hour block of shifts went by, but it didn't seem to matter because the three didn't mind sharing time slots

with each other. It came to the 1 AM shift, which was Freddy's shift. Overall, it was uneventful with no crazy messages from listeners. Nate was a little disappointed by it. They signed off, and everyone logged off to their separate

ways.

Freddy tried to play a computer game to take his mind off everything. He played Doom a lot and loved real-time strategy games. He popped in his favorite real-time strategy game, Age of Empires, and proceeded to try to dominate the world to clear his head. No sooner than his first attack on the neighboring village, he noticed the lights flicker. The computer screen didn't flicker, so it must be a faulty light bulb. He continued to play on. The lights flickered once more, this time with a longer duration before it brightened up again. He assumed someone was messing with the light switch, which was located at the top of the stairs. Freddy turned around in his computer chair. Standing up, he saw what stood before him; a tall, gangly creature. His face was dripping with mucus or saliva, poised in a scowl. The body was dressed in military garb. Beside him on either side, were two dogs in various forms of decay. Their fangs protruded from their mangled jaws. This was it. This

was clearly not a dream. Freddy felt his heart leap into his chest.

As quick as the vision was, it went away. The light stopped flickering, the dogs disappeared, and The General was nowhere to be found.

"Holy shit. Holy shit," Freddy kept saying under his breath, over and over.

How was this possible? This guy on the internet was not kidding. That was the most terrifying thing he had ever seen. Was it even real? It had to be. His mind raced as he tried to figure out a logical reason for what just happened. He tried to pinch himself and do all of the self-check methods to see if you are dreaming, turning up empty. This was reality. This happened.

Freddy didn't sleep at all the entire night. He powered through until daylight. He made his way the first chance he could to the local library. He needed to see if there was anything regarding The General at all. The library would clearly have a book on this guy. He began his walk to the library, through the twists and turns of the neighborhood. It was a grey, gloomy day. Clouds hung low in the sky, with an ominous warning of an impending storm.

Freddy didn't care. He kept on and made his journey.

Once in the library, he immediately looked for a section titled 'Demons' or anything that sounded like it would be helpful. After scanning aisle to aisle and row by row, there was no easy section to find. He did not want to get assistance, because honestly, what would they think? The fewer questions, the better, Freddy decided. Finally, he saw it. A small section, at the bottom far end of an aisle labeled 'Occult and Supernatural.' This had to be the spot. He quickly squatted down and began scanning every title on the shelf. There were books on Wiccan, ghost stories, ancient teachings, and theories, but nothing that said, "Demons Named the General," A break, a small break is all Freddy wanted with this book. There, on the far right-hand side of the row, he saw it. A book called "Demons in the Modern Society, A Guide to Ancient and Modern Forms of Underworld Beings." This had to be it and needed to be because quite frankly, it was the only book fitting of the description. He drew it from the shelf and headed to a reading area.

Thumbing through the book, he read of all the supernatural beings from Hell, or at least as the book described, the human perception of hell. The book described that what we viewed as demons were nothing more than a being from an alternate plane of existence. That didn't ease his mind at all, but maybe it was a nugget of information to store for later. He read on. He was looking for anything; a history, a picture, or even its name. He saw in the movies that if you know the demons' real name it holds power over it. There was nothing. No mention of this being. There was no lore to be found. The only details he knew were from that instant message from the other night, and even that was erratic and crazed at best.

Freddy thought to himself, "What the hell am I going to do?"

Night came as quick as it could, much to the displeasure of Freddy's best desires to remain in the day time. How many days did he have? Was it like that one Japanese movie where he had a week? What were the rules for this? Thoughts raced around his brain rapid-fire, trying to make sense and figure out what was going on. He decided that being online and on the phone with his fellow friends from the radio would help him ease through it. Neither Nate nor Seth could be found online, and that was disappointing. The early evening DJ, Joe, was on. He didn't really talk to Joe much, but they all knew each other, so he figured he would strike up the conversation.

"Hey, did you hear what we were going on about the other night?"

No response from Joe. He must have been in the middle of something because the music was playing. Maybe he hit the restroom or stepped out to smoke. Time passed, and there was still no response from Joe. Freddy needed to distract himself. He fired up his favorite shooter game and powered through the hordes of zombies and demons on Mars.

Five stages into the game, he heard a noise in the back room. The stupid cat was clearly up to something again. He paused the game and hesitantly got up from his chair. Slowly staggering toward the laundry room, he went to fumble for the light. As he grabbed the pull chain, he felt something touch his arm. Looking through the dark room, he couldn't see anything near him, and his heart was racing. Quickly yanking down on the chain, the light fired off right away. There he was. It was. There stood The General, Reaching for Freddy. He tried to run but felt as if his legs were made of rubber. The creature stood before him, as disgusting as before, joined by two hellhounds on either side of him. The demon reached back and thrust his disgusting, gnarled, clawed fist forward, striking Freddy where he stood. It caused him to fly back into the sliding door separating the rooms.

Once Freddy looked up after recovering to his feet, The General once again vanished into the void once more. Freddy walked himself over to the bathroom and checked himself out in the mirror. There was a giant cut across his chin, and his shirt was torn. There was a bit of blood on the center of his shirt, which he noticed was dripping from his nose. He hadn't noticed it in the commotion, but it was pouring blood. Reaching for one of the towels on the rack, he tried to stop the bleeding, but it kept coming. The stain on his shirt grew as he tried to stop the bleeding from his nose. Pain shot through his mouth as well. He felt around with his tongue. His teeth all felt loose and began falling out, one by one.

This was too unreal. Crying, panicking, and breathing heavily, Freddy tried his best to stop everything from happening. Blood began to flow from the corners of his eyes as he wept. The only thing he could do was drop down to the floor and curl in a ball. The light in the bathroom flickered on and off as he knelt to the floor. Doors, cabinets, and drawers slammed open and closed. A full cacophony of sounds filled the room, and he began hearing whispers in his ears. It was all too much, all at once. Freddy screamed out in agony and fear into the darkness. All at once, the noises stopped. The lights steadied. After collecting himself, he looked down and did not see any spots of blood or even his teeth on the floor. His teeth were in the proper place, but they still hurt as if they had been ripped from his skull and shoved back in.

Bewildered and shaken from what had just happened, he turned on the faucet and splashed some water onto his face. Bracing himself for what may happen if he looked into the mirror because he has seen one too many horror movies, Freddy looked at his reflection. It was just him. No cuts. No scrapes. No blood. It was as if everything had been a dream.

No one would ever believe him. How could they? He wondered what time it was because it felt like hours had passed since this whole ordeal transpired. Freddy walked shakily back to the computer and sat down. One minute had passed. How had only one minute passed? After all of that? It may have taken him a minute to clean his face, but all of that torment? As if it never happened? A response came across the messenger. It was Joe.

"Sorry, man, miles away. What's up now? I missed the show the other day."

Freddy sighed and replied, "It was crazy, but don't worry about it."

What if that kid was right? What if telling someone passed the torch to someone else?

"Tell me, man. It's bugging me. Do it!" Joe plead over the chat window. "Fine, but don't say I didn't warn you," He began, preparing Joe for the worst.

"So, this guy apparently haunts you and steals your soul. I just went through a hell of an ordeal like five minutes ago, and I don't even know how to explain it. The crazy part is the psycho fan told me that by telling me all about this demon dude, the curse was lifted from him and was now my problem."

There was no response from the other end for a few moments. The hesitance was picking at Freddy's already distraught nerves.

"Sweet. So, like whatever this is, it's contagious? What is he?" pried Joe.

Freddy dropped his head to the desk. Does he tell Joe? He won't shut up about it. What if he tells multiple people at the same time? Obviously, he was reading the messages aloud to everyone on the air. Surely everyone was affected. He told Joe that he would call Charlie, one of his friends, and tell them both what went down. Using the digital phone system on the computer, he dialed out to Charlie and Joe. Joe picked up, followed by Charlie.

"Man! Freddy has a crazy story to tell! It's this demon thing, and he won't tell me about it. It's lame," Joe ribbed.

Freddy scoffed very audibly on the phone because everything was being made into a joke.

"Ok, come on, shoot. What is it?" Charlie encouraged.

Freddy cleared his throat. He began to speak the same story the guy on the messenger told him.

"Well, after the guy told me all of that, I didn't think it was for real. I was literally too scared out of my wits to even say what happened, but let me say it sucked."

There was silence on the other end of the phone for a moment, but Joe spoke up.

"So, wait, this thing steals your soul? You gotta tell someone the story, and you pass the curse? That how it works?"

Freddy thought for a moment, licked his lips, and croaked out a reply.

"Yea. Basically. I don't know anything about this thing."

Charlie and Joe were silent for another brief pause when suddenly, a yell was heard over the phone.

"Son of a bitch!" It was Joe.

"Wait, you just told us, so does that mean he comes after me and Charlie now? Dude! Not cool!"

Charlie sounded livid. Freddy needed to explain his theory of defeating this curse before he blew his lid entirely.

"Ok, so, a loophole. We read it over the air last night, and no one was really affected. Not the other DJs, listeners, no one. So now that I told the two of you, it should pass from me and just disappear and not do anything. Or, it still haunts me. So, it's still my problem. I just need to talk to someone, and you guys were the only ones I could think of."

Joe sighed hard on the phone, breathing into the microphone as he did, causing a lot of wind interference.

"Ok, well, that makes sense, I guess. You know we got your back, and we can try to look up what we can about this demon thing. I'll check at the college near me tomorrow. Charlie, what are you going to get into?" There was silence on the phone.

"Charlie? Chuckster? Charles in Charge?"

Joe prodded for a response, but there was nothing on the other end.

"Shit, did he disconnect?" asked Freddy.

"God. What have you done? Was I the only one to hear it? How much did he hear? When did he cut out?"

Joe panicked hard, and his mind clearly raced with thoughts as to if this was real or a joke.

"Dude, you gotta be kidding me, man!"

Joe hung up the phone loud and angrily. Freddy sat in his chair in disbelief. Does this thing really transfer to him? Would the curse be removed, and bounce over to Joe since Charlie was not listening to the story? Freddy felt horrible about what just happened, but in the back of his mind, he was completely relieved.

Freddy woke up the next day, feeling a bit different. He didn't feel like there was an ominous presence clouding up his head. He still felt remorseful about what happened. He called Charles to ask if he disconnected. No answer, which was strange. Going into work felt odd, and everything felt meaningless, but at the same time it was a relief to be doing work. It helped clear his head and keep busy. He wondered what happened to Charlie and what was going to happen to Joe if this thing transferred to him. The shift end came quickly. Before Freddy knew it, he was back home. He was ready to broadcast on the radio once again. Freddy tried to call Joe before getting started.

The phone rang a half ring and picked up. No one said anything on the other end, so Freddy decided to speak up.

"Yo!"

There was some shuffling on the other side, followed by heavy breathing.

"Joe?"

Freddy tried his hardest to get him to speak up.

"I know you're there."

There was more shuffling and, finally, a voice.

"H-Hello? Freddy?"

It was Joe. He sounded shaken. He knew exactly what that tone was. He knew that level of fear.

"You ok? What's going on?" Freddy questioned, knowing the answer was obvious.

"It's him. The General. He's coming for my soul! Freddy, I know it! He's here, haunting me, and his hellhounds are barking outside. I can't even do this right now."

Freddy was helpless to do anything for him. He tried to offer any consoling, but it went nowhere.

"Dude, don't patronize me! You did this to me! He's in my house. I'm hiding right now, but I'm freaking out. I saw him. The General. I saw him."

Joe began to describe exactly what he saw to Freddy in vivid detail. Freddy knew exactly what he was seeing, and that image was burned into his brain. Then it happened. Silence. Did it get Joe? There wasn't any screaming, and there should be screaming, because he would be screaming. "You good, dude?" Freddy asked, not prepared for the answer. There was noise over the phone, shuffling and banging.

After a few moments, Joe spoke.

"Yeah. Yeah, I think I'm good. I don't know dude, like, he was gonna get me and then didn't. Now everything is back to normal. The blood on my walls is gone. The window isn't broken anymore from the hellhound. My bed is back to normal. The lights, they're all on and working. There's nothing. What the hell just happened?"

Freddy had no idea how this thing worked. Does it just spook you for a while and grabs you when you're most vulnerable? He's seen enough scary movies to deduce what should happen, but this was real life.

"Well, I guess it's over, Joe," Freddy said as he played on his computer, checking his messenger and email.

There was a new email from Charles, and he clicked the link. It was sent out shortly after the phone call, according to the date and time.

Freddy,

Dude, my bad about earlier. I guess the phone got cut off, Dad didn't pay the bill or something. I'll hit you up once it's back up and running. I wanted to tell you to NOT go on with the story without me. I don't even know if you knew I was off the phone, so I wanted to email you about it. Fill me in dude.

Charles.

He didn't hear the story because his phone didn't work? That's crazy. He stretched back in his chair for a moment and cupped his hands to his face and let out a small yell. He took a deep breath and opened his eyes back up. He looked around his room, still not believing everything that went on. He decided to type out an email response to Charles and fill him in on everything.

Charles,

Dude. I told Joe. I told Joe everything. I didn't know you weren't on the phone, so I think It's after him. He told me it stopped at his house just now. So, this thing, it's a big nasty dude, named The General, in case you wanted to look him up. He haunts you and eventually steals your soul for whatever reason. He has some hellhounds with him. Big, nasty dogs, missing skin and glowing eyes, the whole nine yards. He only comes after you if you're cursed, and the only way to transfer the curse is to tell someone about it. Since it's on Joe right now, don't listen to the story if he tells you because if he tells you, it's your problem. Glad you're ok, though.

Freddy.

He proofread a bit to make sure there were no spelling errors or crazy typos. As he finished proofreading his email, there was a loud noise from behind him. The damn cat was clearly knocking something down, and Freddy was over it already. He spun the chair to the side to throw a sock at the cat when it happened. There, in the corner of his room, smiling with a yellow, sharp-toothed grin, stood The General. At his sides were his two faithful pups growling with saliva dripping from their jowls.

Freddy screamed a blood-curdling scream as he pointed his gnarled, mangled finger toward Freddy. At that command, the two hellhounds leaped for him. The first bit down its fangs into Freddy's left calf, the pain completely unbearable. The second bit down on his foot and got nothing but shoe on the first bite.

The General started to walk towards him. How was this possible? How did this happen? He thought the curse was lifted. What was going on? He remembered as the dog on his left side began ripping flesh from his calf muscle, in the haze of this torment, he didn't send the email. He reached around and placed his hand on the mouse. He moved the cursor over to the send button. A painful hot scratch ripped down his back, from his neck to the side of his ribs. The General was now upon him. All three began to ravenously rip the flesh from Freddy. His vision blurred and began to fade. The pain began to fade, and he knew he was going to die. Tears were in his eyes as he tried hopelessly to fight back with what he had left of his body. One of the hellhounds reached his mouth toward Freddy's neck, biting down.

The life blinked out of Freddy moments later.

As his body went limp, his hand dropped onto the mouse, clicking the send button. A second later, the screen read "Message Sent."

The End

What Really

Happened:

A little background on this story. Way back in the golden years of 2004, I used to DJ on an online radio station. This was ages before Podcasts were mainstream. We were live and pretended to be like the FM stations. We did the standard blabber between songs, played requests, and of course, in some form, we spoke to listeners.

We spoke to these people through AOL Instant Messenger back in its heyday. We had normal chats with these guys. They would tell tales of funny news, regurgitate jokes back to us, and of course, they would tell us which songs to play. Pretty standard fare in a typical shift.

I ran the late-night shift, from midnight to three in the morning. I would usually be joined by the two previous DJs, and we would make it a party. On a particular night, some listener started messaging me while songs were playing. He made small talk, as they always did. Eventually, things took a crazy left turn.

He started asking if I believed in demons and the supernatural. I dismissed it, more or less, but I let him continue. He started telling me about this demon who haunted him, The General, and how it plagued him nightly. He described visually what he saw. He went on with this story for a few more paragraphs of text, then hit me with the crazy part. Speaking to someone else about it transfers the curse to that person.

I couldn't believe it. Let me tell you, my next three nights were severely sleepless. I kept hearing noises in the basement, and I slept with the lights on for a while. I shared with a friend, and it freaked him out as well. We ended up writing a song about it, and I felt the story was crazy. Hopefully, you enjoyed this embellishment on the sort of true story that happened in my life to inspire this tale.

2

Demon Dog

R obin was your average tomboy. She enjoyed playing with action figures, getting dirty in the mud, and playing physical sports. She was small, with long blonde hair, and always wore pop culture t-shirts. She loved movies but didn't understand most of them being only eight years old. She was always into whatever her dad was into, which were classic cult movies from the 80s decade mostly. She had plenty of friends who all went to her elementary school and lived a fairly average life for what could be considered average in the early 1990s.

After returning home from school one regular, mundane day, she retired to her room to play with her newly acquired dinosaur toys, based on the latest movie that released. She had a small room with a bed in the far corner, directly across from the bedroom door and diagonally from the closet door. Robin had a bunch of stuffed animals stashed away in nets hanging above the bed and a nice writing desk to complete homework. The curtains were Winnie the Pooh design, and a special night light switch with Mickey Mouse adorned the wall by the door.

Dinner was served promptly at 6 pm, and Robin was delighted to enjoy tonight's meal; baked chicken and macaroni with cheese, her favorite. Her dad would always try to sneak a green vegetable on her plate.

"Daddy, I'm not eating this yucky nastiness," she said as she scraped the green beans to the far side of the plate, away from the rest of the food. "Well, you'll learn to love them as you get older, I can tell you that.

I didn't like them as a kid either," her father said, trying to bond as a means to get her to eat the beans.

Robin helped clean the dishes, and the two settled in the living room to watch a movie. It was raining outside, so playing out there was not in the cards. Tonight's entertainment was some Kurt Russell film about some truck driver, her dad's favorite. She didn't really understand the movie, but it seemed interesting enough with the fight scenes. She lay across the couch, and before you knew it, during the climax of the final scenes, Robin began to nod off.

Robin jolted awake, realizing she nodded off. Her dad was looking down at her, smiling.

"Ok, that's enough movie for you tonight. Go brush your teeth and get ready for bed. I'll tuck you in soon."

With that, he gave her a kiss on the forehead and patted her along towards the upstairs bathroom. Groggily climbing the stairs, Robin made her way up, winding the 90-degree turn and going up the rest of the stairs to the top.

Robin was ready for bed after brushing her teeth, washing her face, and hands. She headed to her room just around the corner, changed into her Ninja Turtle pajamas, and climbed into bed. She had a diverse love for all of the cartoons on television, but the turtles were one of her favorites. It was Thursday, so it was Turtle Thursday.

Making sure her stuffed animals were in order, she scooted down into the covers. The sun was finally set outside, which she could clearly see through the window that overlooked the alleyway. Her dad came in to tuck Robin in, as promised. He completed his usual routine of saying goodnight to each and every animal in the room by name and then finally tucking Robin in with a kiss on the forehead.

"Goodnight pumpkin head," he said as he started to turn for the door.

"Daddy?" She asked sleepily.

"What is it, sugarplum?"

"Daddy, can you close the closet? I forgotted to do it."

24

Her dad looked over at the partially open closet door. They were folding closet doors, double doors. He walked over to the one that was ajar and pushed it closed.

"Good? Anything else?" he asked, waiting to see if there was anything else before leaving.

"Nope. Ready for bed, captain!"

He smiled and slowly closed the door behind him, leaving it open a crack.

Robin was brave, but she still needed the door open a crack. She didn't like it all the way opened because from where she slept, you could see all the way down the hallway. It was something she didn't want to wake up in the middle of the night to see, and it was especially hard to fall asleep looking down the hallway as well. The hallway light flicked off, and she heard her father make his way downstairs, probably to watch more tv or a movie. She closed her eyes and drifted off to sleep.

Robin was awoken in the middle of the night by a noise she had never heard before. It sounded like growling or something, kind of like the big T-Rex dinosaur in that movie before he roars at the family. The moonlight filled the room, and she could see well in the dark. There was nothing in the room, and she assumed it may have been her dog, Chipper. He was a little Yorkie but was fat and had breathing problems. Maybe that was him because he makes funny noises all the time.

She scanned the room and listened for his dog tag to clink, but there was nothing. Slowly, she sat up from the bed to get a better look. The closet door was slightly opened. She knows it was closed earlier; she saw it get closed. Robin considered not getting out of bed, but it was going to bother her if she didn't fix it. Maybe she could go to the bathroom and make it worth the trip out of her warm, soft bed.

She slowly climbed out of bed, placing both feet on the floor. Carefully navigating the floor in the dark, she reached for the closet door. Once her hand touched the knob, the gurgling sound stopped. In fact, all sound stopped entirely and was replaced by a sharp ringing in her head. Her eyes started to bother her too. They began to see stars, only faintly at first but started to intensify. She pulled the knob to try to close it, and at once, both doors flew open.

There in the depths of the closet, something was waiting. She didn't quite know, nor could she really see what it was. What she could see were two brightly glowing red eyes looking at her from the shadows. She gasped and began to step backward from the closet. Her vision was still obscured. She couldn't see what it was, but it looked mean. The shadow of this thing was massive. Robin tried to scream, but her voice was stifled. She couldn't scream.

The creature leaped at Robin. As it connected with her body, claws digging into her shoulders, she woke up. Her heart was racing. She was screaming but doesn't remember doing it, but she continued to scream. Loud thuds came from beyond her bedroom door, and the door burst open, and lights flicked on.

"What?! What?! What?! What's wrong, honey?" Her father said, sitting down on the bed to wrap his arms around her.

"I-I-I had a bad d-dream!" she said, still trembling, and making out words through her sobbing and sniffling.

"Well it's over now, you're ok. Do you want to tell me about it?" Her father sat back a bit to listen.

"I-I-I," she couldn't get the words out, she needed to cry good and hard before anything worthwhile was coming out.

"Holy smokes, what happened to your PJs? Have they always had the hole?" he asked, grabbing the pajama top at the should and looking closely, pulling at the fabric.

Robin looked down at her shirt. Sure enough, there were a few tiny rips across each shoulder, just in front. They were exactly where the monster got her in her dream. She cried harder because these were her favorite pajamas. Her dad just let it all come out and held her until she was able to compose herself.

"How you doing, champ?" he asked, trying to console her.

"Better," she said.

After calming down enough and clearing the tears from her face, Robin was ready to speak.

"Daddy, it was scary. There was a monster in the closet, and I couldn't hear anymore. I couldn't see anymore, and-and-and," she started choking up again.

"It's ok, monsters aren't real. They just make them in movies, and they're fake. No more scary movies for you before bed, young lady. Now, let's get you cleaned up in the bathroom and back to bed. It's past midnight."

Her dad helped Robin to get up, and he planned to carry her in his arms to the bathroom. She climbed into his arms, and he turned and started for the door. Out of the corner of his eye, he noticed something.

"Hmm, the closet door must be busted. I'll take a look at it tomorrow," and the two went off to the bathroom.

Robin rinsed her face with water and calmed down. The two walked back to the bedroom, and her dad went over to close the closet. He played with the door a few times to check it, and it seemed in decent order.

Robin was still on edge as she climbed back into the bed. She adjusted her stuffed animals that were against the wall and nestled back under the covers. "Daddy, can you leave the hallway light on, please?" Her father looked at her and smiled.

"Sure. If you feel better with it on, I'll leave it on. Goodnight, princess."

He flipped off the bedroom light and left the room. He closed the door, leaving it open only slightly to leave the light to creep into the room. Robin still had tears running down her cheeks. It was the most terrifying dream she ever had, and she thought that it was very real. Her pajamas were torn. The closet door was open, it had to have happened. The only thing she didn't understand was that she was standing by the window in front of the closet, and she woke up in the bed. Either way, it was still very scary for her. She tried to close her eyes to get to sleep and prepare to go to school tomorrow.

The next morning the rain had stopped. The ground was wet with puddles, and the sun had not shone quite yet to clear it up. Robin ate breakfast with her dad, who made pancakes and bacon.

"Did you sleep any better, sweetie?" he asked as she rounded the corner toward the dining room table.

"I dunno," she replied coyly.

"Well, no more bad dreams, ok? Can't have bad dreams with bacon in your belly!"

She smiled at the joke and began to eat her breakfast. The bus would be at her corner any minute, and she didn't want to be late. After finishing her plate, she took it to the sink and gave her dad a hug. He grabbed her backpack and passed it to her. She put on her jacket, and they started for the door.

"You'll be fine. You have your friends and me. You're super brave, and no big bad nightmare can hurt you, because I'll hurt them first."

He made a karate pose and started chopping at the air. Robin giggled at how silly her dad was, and it honestly made her feel much better.

At school, Robin sat through Mrs. Nelson's class. She was such a fun teacher and always had a way with the kids. Today they were learning about planets and the solar system. She was excited to learn this subject, as she loved all things science and science fiction. Today they were learning about Mars, and it's two moons. Two moons were an exciting concept for Robin since she could only see one moon. The class colored a picture of Mars and wrote down a few facts they learned about Mars underneath the image. They proudly went to the hallway to hang them on display for the school to see.

Everyone returned to the class and sat down.

Mrs. Nelson asked the class, "Now, did anyone draw aliens or any Martian monsters?"

The class laughed a bit.

School ended at 2:45, and everyone grabbed their bags and headed for the doors. Robin stayed behind. She wanted to ask Mrs. Nelson a question, so she walked to her desk.

"Line up at the door, Robin. We are going to walk to the playground for dismissal."

"I wanted to ask you a something, Mrs. Nelson," Robin shyly asked her teacher.

"Ok, let's go downstairs to line up, and we can talk there."

Robin nodded and got in her place in line. The class walked down to the playground, where parents picked up their children or were loaded onto the bus by administration and staff. Robin tugged on Mrs. Nelson's sweater.

"Oh, I almost forgot, sweetheart. What is it you wanted to say?" Mrs. Nelson knelt down to speak to Robin.

"Oh, umm, I wanted to ask if you ever had a bad dream?"

Mrs. Nelson's facial expression changed to serious for a moment, but then returned to a smile.

"Well, Robin, everyone has bad dreams. They happen. It is your brain playing a movie for you to watch while you are asleep. Sometimes it plays a happy, funny movie. Sometimes, it plays a sad movie. But, there are those times we all do not like, that it plays a scary movie. That is what a nightmare is, sweetie, a scary movie."

Robin stood there for a moment, trying to process this whole concept. "What if the movie hurts you in real life, though?" Robin asked.

Mrs. Nelson raised an eyebrow.

"What do you mean, 'if it hurts you in real life?' Are you ok?"

Mrs. Nelson stood to her feet and began looking around the playground, a concerned look on her face was apparent.

"I am okays, but I had a bad dream and I woked up and my pajammies were torn. And that is where I got hurted in my dream."

Mrs. Nelson held Robin's hand as she walked her to the bus stop. "So, you had a dream, and the dream hurt you when you were awake? They can't do that, honey. They are not real."

Robin did not seem amused by this answer. "NO! It is real, and it really hurt and I am scared to go to sleep!"

Mrs. Nelson stopped. She turned to Robin and looked down.

"Ok. You don't live too far away, so I'll tell you what. I'll check with someone, and I will give you a ride home. I need to talk to your father about this. He is obviously letting you watch those scary movies again."

"Oh no, daddy isn't home yet. And he didn't let me watch a scary movie last night! We watched some movie with a guy fighting someone with lightning shooting out of his hands! Promise!" She pleaded because she did not want her father in trouble.

"Ok, well, if this is still a problem on Monday, you tell me first thing, okay? I want you to be ok. It's my job to protect you kids," Mrs. Nelson said as she escorted Robin to her bus.

Robin boarded the bus and sat down at her usual seat in the back by the window. She pulled the window down and said goodbye to her teacher. Mrs. Nelson gave a faint wave and turned toward the school. The bus, fully loaded, began its journey to drop off the children.

Robin was one of the last stops on the route. It took over two hours to get to the end of the line because one kid requested to be dropped off at a different location. The bus driver was not allowing it. The bus pulled over to phone the parents to confirm the different location. Once that was sorted out, driving resumed. By the time Robin arrived home, her father was just pulling up to the house. He drove a blue Pinto with wood paneling on the side and did construction work. He always had lumber and tools in the back of the trunk. He got out of the car and waved to Robin as she walked down the sidewalk. She started to run toward her father and leaped to give him a giant hug.

"Welcome home, bug! What's the plan for tonight? We have the weekend off. Are we going to be party animals?" he asked.

The idea of this weekend has been in talks for weeks. Her father typically worked weekends, so the fact the two of them had the same days off was exciting. They went into the house to get cleaned up because tonight they were going to the Fun Zone. Robin was going to have a blast playing on all of the obstacle courses. After showering and changing clothes, the two were ready to hit the town. They ate pizza, played video games, and Robin even got to ride a zip line. This was the most fun she has had in a while, and she didn't even think about the nightmare anymore.

They returned home around 9 PM, past Robin's bedtime. She quickly ran upstairs, brushed her teeth, and changed into her pajamas. This time it was her Slimer ones, with slime that used to glow at night. After several washes, however, the design no longer glowed. Even if they didn't work anymore, she still liked them. She rode the stairs down on her butt as she went downstairs, still keyed up from all the excitement that happened tonight. The two of them
watched a boring television show, and Robin began to nod off on the couch. Her father saw, carried her up to bed, and tucked her in. He said goodnight to the stuffed animal gang, and turned off the light, closing the door only slightly. He left the hallway light on and retreated back downstairs to watch TV.

The wind howled a bit outside. There must be another storm coming, Robin thought, but drifted off to sleep. There was a noise in the house that woke her from her sleep. The hallway light was on, and the door completely open. She was positive her dad closed it when he left. She got out of bed and grabbed the doorknob. That was when she heard it. The growling, the crazy noise she heard last night. Her ears began to ring as they did the previous night. She turned to make her way to her bed, and as she turned, her vision began to blur and white-out, like before.

There, at the foot of her bed, she saw movement. She couldn't make out much, but there was movement. She tried to make it to her bed, but the creature crawled around the bed. She had nowhere to go. All Robin wanted to do was to climb under the covers and make all of this go away. She made a dash for the bed. She doesn't know why, but it felt like a safe place to be. As she darted for the bed, the creature leaped up and landed on the bed, sliding it slightly away from the wall. The growling was growing even louder, and the ringing did not stop. Robin thought quickly how to get out of this situation and turned to run down the hallway. She made it to the top of the stairs. The monster was standing in the doorway of her bedroom, growling and snarling. She was able to get a good look at it. It was a large, muscly built, dog-shaped monster. It looked evil. Its skin was brown and leathery. Its eyes were glowing red. Its teeth were sharper than anything she had ever seen. It began a pounce in her direction. Robin didn't know what to do, and she jumped from the top of the stairs to the bottom.

Before hitting the wall at the landing, Robin shot up from her bed. She was sweating, crying, and breathing hard, unable to comprehend what was happening. Her father came running in after all of the commotions and flipped on the light.

"What's wrong? What's going on?" he said, rushing to her bedside.

"The monster, daddy! The monster again!"

She sobbed uncontrollably. He looked around the room. The bed was in disarray, almost a foot from the wall it was pushed against. Her stuffed animal nets were ripped from the wall, tearing up the drywall on their exit.

"You know I have to fix those walls," he said, slightly angrily.

"I'm sorry, daddy, but I didn't do it! It was the monster doggie!" He sat down on the bed.

"Monster doggie?"

Robin sat up, wiping the tears from her eyes.

"Yeah. Monster doggie. He was super scary. I was so scared, and I jumped downstairs."

"Well, I'm sure I would have seen you hit the wall downstairs if you did. It's just a bad dream. You must have been flailing around because you knocked this bed all over. Calm down, sweetie. You'll be fine."

With that, he tucked her in and kissed her goodnight once more. He turned off the light and closed the door slightly behind him, leaving the hallway light on as he made his way downstairs. Robin tried to drift back off to sleep, trying to ignore what happened.

The next morning, Robin made her way down to the living room. Her father was working in the basement, grabbing tools to repair the wall from last night, probably. Breakfast had not been made, and she was hungry. Pouring a bowl of her favorite sugar-filled cereal, she watched Saturday morning cartoons. A few moments into the episode, her father came upstairs with a handful of tools. He set them down in the recliner in the corner of the room near the front door across from the stairway.

"Morning sunshine," he said, dusting his hands off.

"Good morning, daddy. Want to watch cartoons?" she said as she pointed to the brightly colored characters on screen.

He waved his hand.

"No, because someone in this house flailed around and pulled half of the wall down. I now have to patch up the holes and rehang your nets."

He sighed as he collected his tools and went upstairs. Robin felt horrible about last night and wanted to make things right. She took her cereal bowl to the sink and went upstairs to lend a hand. Her dad was setting up a step ladder as she came into the room.

"Can I help? I'm sorry everything is broke."

He smiled at her.

"Sure. Do me a favor, open the window since it's nice out."

Robin walked over and raised the window up, and the gentle breeze fluttered in.

"Ok, now I'm going to need you to hand me that right there."

He pointed to the putty knife on the floor. She grabbed it for him and passed it up to him.

"Ok, the next part is really important. I need you to hold this cup for me, so I can fill up these holes in the wall." He had her hold the cup of spackle.

"I'm not upset with you. I want you to know that," he started, "I just don't understand why you'd make up such a story."

He filled the first hole and smoothed out the surface. Robin held up the spackle, so he could fill the second hole.

"But I-" she stopped.

She figured it was better to drop the subject than keep trying to bring it up.

"Thank you for fixing my wall."

The last hole was filled up, and her dad climbed down from the ladder. He set down the putty knife and took the spackle from Robin. He took a knee in front of her.

"Listen. We are going to stop watching these movies until we get your bad dreams under control."

The two cleaned up the mess, pushed the bed back, and made the bed. Robin made sure every stuffed animal was in its right place.

"Do you want to go get some ice cream?"

Robin nodded. She was glad things were ok, and her dad wasn't mad at her. "Well, get cleaned up, and we will head out," he said, collecting his tools.

Robin showered and got dressed for ice cream in record time. The two hopped in the station wagon and headed off to get ice cream. The day time was a better time for Robin, but the last two nights were miserable. It was nice to break her mind from everything that was going on. After a day at the mall, the two headed home.

On the drive home, her dad made small talk.

"Well, you know, later tonight we can make dinner. What do you want to eat?"

"How about a quesadilla?" Robin excitedly asked.

"Hmm, Spanish food. But you're sure you can eat a whole case? Why not try one dilla and see how you feel," he joked, in his worst dad joke he could muster up.

Robin didn't get it. They listened to hair band metal on the radio station and sang along to a lot of the music. The mall wasn't far from the house, so they were home in no time. Dinner was prepared, and Robin put the dishes into the sink. She went to play in her room for a bit. There was some dinosaur action calling her name. It was four in the afternoon, so she wasn't thinking of anything negative.

Making the velociraptors eat the scientists grew tiresome, and she put the toys away in their case. Robin sat in her writing chair at her desk and started to try to color something but started to nod off. She shook her head awake, but she knew she was not sleeping the past few nights. It was going to catch her. She may as well fall asleep in the daytime, right? She laid her head down on the desk, arms folded underneath, and before she knew it, she fell fast asleep. She woke up at her desk soon after. She wasn't sure what time it was, but it was already night outside. The moon was out and full, shining brightly through the alley window. Robin rubbed her eyes and straightened out her back by stretching. She must have been asleep for hours. Robin had a clock in her room, a Nickelodeon clock that made crazy sounds for the alarms. It was blinking 12:00 over and over. It must have reset. She decided to go see what her dad was up to, as he was usually up late watching TV and movies.

She stood from the canvass chair, pushed it back in under the desk, and headed for her bedroom door. It was dark in the room, but there was a glow of light from underneath the door. The moon shone enough light to show the way. When she reached for the doorknob, she heard the familiar sound she had been dreading all day. The growling sound of the demon dog that has been tormenting her the past few nights. It came from the closet. She glanced over at the closet and saw the sliding doors slowly creeping open, as the growling grew louder. She knew jumping into the bed was a bad idea.

The only way through this was to get downstairs.

She ripped open the door as the demon dog burst through the open closet doors, crashing into the writing desk on the way out. She looked at it. It was as terrifying as before. This time, her vision did not blur. She could hear everything, especially the growling. Looking at it clear as day, she could see the leathery skin glistening with slime, or maybe a sweat. Its teeth were protruding from its jaw. Its eyes were red, glowing with a faint yellow spot inside the pupil area. It had pointy ears and two tiny horns on its head. She got a good look but realized it best to take off. She dashed for the top of the stairs across the hallway.

She made it to the top of the stairs, gripped the railings, and looked back one last time. The dog was in the doorway, in a pounce position. She had to get out of there. Her heart was racing, but she knew if she wanted to get out of this, she needed to be a brave girl. She had to be smarter than this thing, just like that kid in her dinosaur movie. She took two steps down the stairs, and the dog leaped at her, crashing into the wall behind her. She did the only thing she could think of to save time: she jumped down the stairs. As her feet left the stairs, she felt a sudden feeling of regret. As her legs were flowing freely in the air, she braced herself to crash into the wall. She also thought it may end up like last time; being a dream and waking up before hitting the wall.

She slammed into the wall with a huge thud and collapsed to the floor. The breath was knocked from her, and she scrambled to get to her feet. She looked around the living room. It was cloaked in a purple haze, and everything seemed surreal. She had to catch her breath for a second and closed her eyes, but only for a moment. She didn't hear the growling behind her, but she needed to get to safety. Maybe to a neighbor's house? She thrust open the front door and ran outside to the front yard, crashing through the gate to the sidewalk. Robin looked up and down the street, terrified. Everything seemed normal outside. There was nothing wrong. Everything was ok. Had she gotten to safety? Was it all in her head? She saw her dad down a few houses, talking to one of the neighbors. She ran to the two of them, completely shaken. They could see the fear in her eyes. Dad decided to ask the obvious question to see what was wrong.

Robin recounted everything that just happened. She woke up, the evil doggie was after her again, and it was mean. She pointed back at their house and said that it was inside the house. He noticed she had a giant bruise on her forehead and some on her arms.

"Are you ok? What happened?" her father asked.

He took Robin by the hand and told the neighbor he would be back in a few after checking on things. They walked together into the threshold of the house. Robin hesitated momentarily, wondering if the dog would be waiting for her on the other side of the door. She stepped inside, there was nothing wrong. Nothing appeared out of place. Her dad went to the stairs and saw a giant crack in the drywall where Robin's little body slammed into it, presumably from the top of the stairs.

"Did you jump down the stairs? No wonder you got bruises all over yourself. You have to stop playing these games!"

Her father was livid. He didn't want to be doing home repairs all weekend.

This was supposed to be a relaxing weekend.

Robin was put to bed soon after cleaning up any mess she made on the way out of the house. She helped fix the front gate and vacuumed up any pieces of wall and debris on the stairs. It was exhausting not being able to sleep, but even more exhausting knowing school was tomorrow. Her father tucked her in, said goodnight to all the stuffed animals, and went down to finish cleaning up the wall. She fell asleep and slept through the night. It was a relief to have an uneventful night.

The next morning, she went off to school without issue. During recess, Robin decided to approach Mrs. Nelson about what had happened all weekend.

"Mrs. Nelson, I had the bad dreams again. I was ascared, and I know you said that dreams can't hurt me, but this one did."

Mrs. Nelson had noticed the bruising on Robin's head and arms but only took note and was going to speak to her about it after school. She knelt to Robin.

"Robin, honey, who hurt you? Is there something you need to tell me?"

Robin waved to her to come closer.

"It's the evil doggie in my room. He chased me again, and I hit the wall hard. I'm ascared."

"Mmhm," Mrs. Nelson responded. "Listen, the next time your doggie monster comes after you, you call the police. Do you know how to dial 911?" Robin nodded.

"Good, because that is what you do if this happens again to you tonight, you hear?"

Mrs. Nelson hugged Robin and went off to watch the rest of the playground.

The class ended, and the school bus dropped her off at the house. Her father was home early. She could see the car out front. Entering the home, she smelled dinner already made, which was nice. The wall had been repaired slightly. She noticed on the way through the living room.

"I'll have to pull out the entire wall and fix that, you know," her dad yelled from the kitchen.

Dinner was silent and very awkward. Nobody said a word the entire time. After her meal, Robin went upstairs to her room to do her homework and prepared for bed. If this monster was going to come out, she was going to be ready to call the police, as Mrs. Nelson said.

She brushed her teeth, put on her pajamas, and headed off to bed. Her father didn't come in for quite some time. Eventually, he came in, tucked her in bed, and left the room. He didn't say goodnight to every animal in the room, which slightly upset Robin. She moved past it and worked to fall asleep. The room was a little darker for some reason this night. The wind was still. There was no rain, but it was probably cloudy since the moon did not shine into the room as always. Robin woke up around 2 AM. She felt something was off and looked around. Her closet door was wide open. She heard growling but did not see the dog. Before she could start to get out of bed to run for safety, the bed began to drift toward the closet. She screamed as loud as she could, but her father did not burst into the room.

This was the most terrifying nightmare she had had. She was paralyzed to move from the bed, and it was slowly floating toward the closet. After a few moments, she was face to face with the entrance of the closet. In the back depths of her closet, she could see two glowing eyes. She had tears in her eyes and could not stop screaming. No one was coming to save her, and she knew this. She had to go through with this dream in order to wake up from it. Suddenly, the bed pitched forward slightly, and she floated into the closet.

The closet doors slammed behind her, and everything went dark.

The next morning, Robin's father was talking to a few police officers.

"Listen. I don't know where she is. Please find my little girl. I don't know where she could have gone," he told the officer who was taking notes.

He sat on the couch quietly as they searched the entire house.

"She's not in the house! Don't you think I would have seen her myself? Start doing your jobs!" he pleaded.

A few moments later, an officer came through the front door.

"O'Malley, you'll want to take a look at this," The officer speaking to Robin's father left to go outside.

"We were just at the school, and her teacher had a lot to tell us. She said she believes Robin was being abused. She came to school with several bruises in the last few days, and she was really scared of something. It checks out with what Parker found upstairs as well as on the landing. Looks like the broken drywall wasn't just something he couldn't explain. We have a decent explanation. Do you want to call it in, or should I?"

Robin's father sat on the couch, retracing the actions that took place over the weekend. He kept thinking of anything that could be a clue from what she was talking about with this demon dog thing. It obviously terrified her, so what could have happened? Where did she hide? He got off the couch to investigate himself. He headed upstairs and rounded the corner to the hallway. Walking closer to her bedroom door, it was surreal to know that she was not in there and may not be in there ever again if the cops didn't start doing something. He opened the door and stepped inside. It was a haze. He could barely think of what was going on as his mind raced on possible places she went. He checked under the bed and walked over to the window. It wasn't opened, and the screen was not out of place. She didn't take the window.

Then, all at once, he remembered. The closet. He remembered closing the closet so many times. Robin said it's where that stupid dog thing came from. He stood up and walked upstairs toward the closet. He made it into the room, hand out, reaching for the doorknob. Suddenly, a handcuff was latched across his wrist.

"Sir, you have the right to remain silent."

They pulled his arm behind him and cuffed it to his other arm. He was escorted out of the bedroom and placed into a squad car just outside.

"The closet! Check the closet!" he yelled.

"We checked the closet. There were a ton of clothes and toys. Obvious scratch marks on the inside of the closet. You disgust me, sir."

They shoved the door closed. The car drove off, lights and sirens blaring, filling the streets with a screaming howl of their sound. The rain began to fall once again.

The End.

The Real Story

O k, so wow, that was a bit much. I wrote the ending and was even surprised myself, wondering where my brain went to pull that darkness out. This was a true story, and I was in the position of Robin. It is only true, up to the fact that the dreams felt super real to me. I couldn't do anything about them. Rather than it lasting a weekend, I dealt with these dreams for almost 12 years of my life. I figured once I was an adult or at least a teenager, it would cut out. It didn't.

I attribute this demon dog to the fact my dad had me watch a ton of 80s movies. There was one movie, in particular, Ghostbusters. That scared the bejeezus out of me. The Terror Dogs terrified me, apparently, even though I could watch the movie on repeat as a child. I was totally into everything they did and never grew out of it. I dress like a Ghostbuster as an adult as well and work in a charity organization group of them. So, it still confuses me to this day how a movie that I love so much could plant a seed of terror in my brain.

My dreams would usually play out one of several ways. I'd get chased out of my bedroom by the dog, only to be struck down leaving the room. I'd wake up screaming, and my mom or dad would come to check on me. The Mickey Mouse night light switch wasn't enough to brighten the room, but they did leave the hallway light on a few times for me, which was cool.

One particular dream I remember I was at the top of the stairs, tying my shoe, and the dog stepped into view from my bedroom. I freaked and leaped down the stairs, waking up before impact with the wall on the landing below. I had two or three dreams in which my bed took off in flight and sailed right into the closet. The last dream I remember having about any of this was that I was lying in bed, and the closet opened as it did in the story. I sat up and decided I was over this before it started. I hopped out of bed, jumped down the stairs, and landed on the landing. I never made it that far before as the dream usually ended then.

The living room was a haze and looked super crazy. Everything was creepy and cast in a purple, hazy, swirly glow. I ran out of the door and found my dad down the street, and he decided to investigate with me. We went inside the house in my dream, and I woke up. I don't even know if it looked normal or if something got us. I never had any more of those dreams after that point. Maybe getting to my dad in time was the game changer my brain needed. But I felt a different ending was in order for this story. Sorry, both of these first two stories had pretty nasty endings, but which was worse? It might be a good idea to stick around for the next one, because I wrote it to be a movie, and never finished that project.

3

Bathell: The Grinning Man

Day 1

The August sun was setting on the Chesapeake Bay, as Tommy finished his beer on his back porch. His home overlooked the scenic landscape over the waters in Annapolis, Maryland. He was your average guy, working a decent 9 to 5 job, and making decent money. He was not married but had a girlfriend, Lisa. Tommy was of average build and usually dressed fashionably when he went out in public. At home, he wore his Texas University hoodies and sweatshirts around. Tommy moved to Maryland a few years ago in order to take a job working on the local military base. He was a proud Texan, displaying the Longhorn fan memorabilia anywhere he could find a shelf. The life he had built was relatively nice. He couldn't complain, he just missed his friends from college.

Tommy pulled his cell phone from his back pocket and scrolled to a contact.

He clicked the icon, 'Maurice,' and began to send a text message.

"Dude, let's set something up while the weather is nice. Bring your girl and anyone else you can think of if they want to fly or a road trip out this way. My house if you all need to crash. You in?" He hit send.

A few moments later, he received a response.

"Bet," Maurice responded that he was in, "When do you think you want to set it up?"

"I'll check with everyone and hit you up when I have something solid. I have a lot of vacay from work I can use."

Tommy smiled. He really was looking forward to this meetup.

Lisa came out from the back door.

"Baby, you going to come inside? It's late."

He hated when his girlfriend did this, but she was so gorgeous, he was always inclined to oblige. He crushed his can in his hand and went inside the house to join his girlfriend. Lisa was your average former cheerleader, late 20 something, went to the local community college, and still enjoyed being physically active. The two met at a local brewery tour, ended up exchanging information, and the rest was history. She loved his exotic accent, but Tommy swears he had no accent. It was her who had the accent, as she was from Baltimore.

Lisa was obsessed with showing Tommy all the movies that were filmed locally. It was almost like a project of hers to find each movie online or in-store and show them off. Tommy just finished off a John Waters movie marathon, which was not half bad. Tonight's movie selection was Runaway Bride, a throwback movie as well. He remembered seeing it ages ago but didn't know it was filmed just across the bay. The couple began the movie, and Tommy felt it was the appropriate time to bring up the question.

"So, Lis, I was thinking. Would it be cool if we had a few people over in a couple of weeks?"

She sat up from the couch.

"Hmm? Like who?"

"Well, a couple of the guys I went to college with back in Texas and their girlfriends. That is if they can make it up here." She reached up and paused the movie.

"Sure, I guess. What's the plan when they get here?"

Tommy thought about that. He didn't consider what the game plan was, outside of hitting a few bars.

"Ooh! I know! What if you gave them the old tourist trip! I could help be the guide!" Lisa excitedly chimed in. "Oh, and I know! We can go to like, the city, and see everything up there, and maybe even down here. We could see the Eastern Shore, and maybe even take a boat tour. Maybe Ocean City and stay, like, in a condo?"

She was very obviously excited about this now.

"Woah! Calm down there, babe. It's only for a couple of days, probably. I want to make sure we don't wear everyone out. Let's see who's in and gauge everyone's interest from there.

Tommy sent out the group text. He reached out to his Texas friends as well as his newer Maryland friends. He wanted to get the groups to intermingle and get to know each other because they all brought something great to the table. Lisa still seemed on the fence about so many people being in the house.

"What if we go camping? Get away from the house and get into nature?" she asked, hoping Tommy would bite.

"Camping? I mean, I guess. RVs or cabins, or are we talking old school tents and a fire type of camping?" Tommy Asked, "I don't get into the camping by a lake either."

"Old fashioned camping. Tents the woods. Nothing but air and trees around us. No water, I know how you get. You don't even like our pool."

Lisa was a very outdoor person and loved nature, so it makes sense for her to suggest something like this.

Tommy updated the message and sent it out.

"Big party: bring your girlfriends or boyfriends. We will hang out at my place and go camping after. Bring camp stuff. Let me know if you can make."

With that, he began the wait to see which friends would want to come out.

Lisa climbed behind Tommy on the couch and put her arms around him.

"See, camping will be fun. Thanks for doing this."

Tommy knew Lisa just didn't want too many people at the house. This was the best way to get them away from it, but at the same time, he was ok with the idea. They would all be at the house a day or two, tops.

The next morning, Tommy received a few responses from friends. Several couldn't make it, but he was delighted to see a hit for the going category. The plan was set, and even though Lisa didn't seem too keen on the idea, he assured her that this was going to be the greatest time they've ever had. Lisa also invited a friend or two of hers along as well. That eased a bit of the feeling she had toward being bombarded by strangers. Tommy knew the weekend was going to be lit.

Lisa spent some time researching a few campgrounds and managed to secure an old fashioned, tent popping patch of dirt. She wanted this since it reminded her of her childhood when they would set up tents and go camping as a family. Tommy agreed on the spot and eagerly awaited the arrival of everyone to their home. He already spent the morning at the sporting goods store picking up everything he could think of; tents, chairs, fire starters, and snacks. He only got the fire-starters because he failed as a boy scout and couldn't light a fire to save his life. He also didn't have time to try to get a fire going in the wild either, not with it possibly being cold at night.

Friday afternoon came quickly for everyone. There was a knock at the door, and Tommy set down his Kindle and made for the door.

"Maurice! My man!"

He gave an elaborate handshake, something that appeared to have been studied and practiced for a few years. Maurice was a tall, stocky black guy, light-skinned, and a wisecracker. He loved to joke, and always played pranks back in their college days in the dorm. Maurice is the type that can't be trusted with a sugar or salt shaker at a restaurant. He will inevitably leave the lid unscrewed for the next guy, but he still had a good heart.

46

"Man, you have no idea how much I hate planes," Maurice said, exhausted from the flight.

He dragged two large suitcases into the house and waved his Uber off that he was good.

"It's been a minute, for real," Tommy nodded in agreement.

"Bro, I can't believe it either. What's it been, four, five years now?" Maurice stood, staring blankly, clearly doing the calculations in his head. "Yeah. Now that you think about it." Lisa walked in from the kitchen.

"Oh, this is my better half, Lisa. Lisa, Maurice."

Maurice did his best curtsy style bow while rolling his hand away from his forehead.

"Charmed, I'm sure, my dear," He said in a pompous accent.

Lisa looked mildly concerned and looked toward Tommy.

"Nah, it's cool. He's just fucking with you, baby."

"Right. Yes, my dear, I do believe it is time for caviar and my afternoon chardonnay," Maurice chimed in, still maintaining the accent.

Everyone paused and looked at each other. Maurice burst out laughing.

"Ok, ok. I can't do it anymore. That was funny as hell. How you doing? So nice to finally meet you!" he said, articulating words through his laughter.

Lisa did not seem amused one bit.

"I guess you can put your stuff in the spare room for now until we get everyone here. Do you want anything to drink?" Maurice smacked his lips.

"You know, I could go for something since my plane didn't believe in having food or drinks on the flight. I guess it pays to pay more for a flight." Lisa smiled.

"Matter of fact, if y'all point me in the general direction, I can sort it all out," Maurice said as he grabbed his luggage.

"Right this way, good sir," Tommy said as he gave his best butler impression, escorting Maurice to the living room area and eventually to the kitchen.

Tommy grabbed a beer for himself and tossed one to Maurice.

"Want to hit the back porch? The view is pretty decent."

Maurice shrugged and started for the back door. The house had a beautiful view of the Chesapeake Bay, which was seen from the large deck built onto the back of the house.

"Damn, son. You did well for yourself. Not bad," Maurice said, sipping from his beer.

"Yeah, It's not too bad. Still needs a lot of work, and the yard is a bitch to maintain," Tommy said, motioning toward the seating that was in front of a fire pit on the deck.

"So, how's life, man? Aside from this house and the lady," Maurice said, adjusting himself in the patio chair.

"Can't complain," Tommy said, leaning forward to turn on the propane fire pit.

"Sure, you can," Maurice jested.

"Well, I just don't feel like I connect with people up here, man. Like, you guys are all I got. After college, I got that job, moved up here, and if not for Lisa, I'd pretty much be alone," Tommy said, adjusting his posture in the chair as he sat down.

"True. If you didn't wear that superhero shirt, I probably wouldn't have said two words to you," Maurice said.

"You told me Batman would beat Superman in a fight with prep time," Tommy laughed.

"But you know I'm right," Maurice beamed, holding his beer out for a cheer clink.

There was a bit of commotion coming from inside the house. Tommy looked back through the sliding door and saw a few faces in the house. They were Lisa's friends; Tiffany, Jeremy, and Janet. They always annoyed Tommy since they had completely different interests, tastes, and attitudes that just got under his skin. Tiffany was a former cheerleader alongside Lisa, trying to live the glory of the olden days while working at the local Applebee's as a shift manager. Jeremy and Janet, however, were on the other side of that profession spectrum. They were each undergraduates studying criminal law and medicine, respectively. Tommy had to go with the flow, as they were all friends since attending middle school.

The sliding glass door opened, and the collection of guests poured out and joined Tommy and Maurice by the fire. Tommy stood up to be polite, reaching his hand out to shake Jeremy's hand.

"How the hell are you guys?" Tommy said, taking a sip of his beer.

"Well, I'm not that bad off actually. We just expanded the kitchen by several square feet, allowing for Tiffany to finally have that island she always wanted," Jeremy gloated.

That was what always bothered Tommy. Jeremy would always have to showcase his latest purchase. A few months ago, at dinner, Jeremy had to brag about the new Lexus he paid for. Tommy was never sure if he had a ton of money or was just an impulse buyer.

"Cool. I'm just over here, drinking my beer, not buying kitchens and islands," Maurice poked, also as his way of introducing himself into the conversation.

"Oh, and this is my good friend, Maurice. Met him down in Texas while I was in college," Tommy said.

"Well, the community college did something for you," Jeremy smiled very smugly.

Maurice could even feel the tension between Jeremy and Tommy but felt best to keep quiet about the matter until later. After introductions were given, plans were to be laid out for the pending camping trip. Tommy didn't like camping and was hesitant on even kicking off this adventure.

Dinner was served at a local restaurant near the water. It was known for its seafood. Tommy and Maurice were not big on the local flavor enhancer, Old Bay. Dinner was a success in Lisa's eyes, as her friends and she were chatting about times in school and memories of the past. However, Maurice and Tommy were sitting at the end of the table, isolated, and feeling like third wheels to the friend brigade. Maurice decided to break the ice, being the outgoing soul he was.

"I'd like to toast to friends, camping, and flying for six hours and still having it in me for dinner."

He held his glass out, but the rest of the table didn't seem amused. Tommy stood up with his glass.

"To friendship and adventures!"

He did his best to liven the mood and interject the duo into the conversation.

Jeremy didn't stand but held his glass up.

"To friendship."

He took a sip from his glass and returned awkwardly to the storytelling. Tommy leaned into Lisa.

"Hey, does Jeremy still have an issue with me?"

She paused and took a long sip from her water glass.

"I don't think so. I mean, we broke up ages ago. He's moved on with Tiffany, I'm sure," Lisa whispered.

Tommy shrugged and resumed eating. The table continued with two separate conversations once again. There was a lot of unspoken tension between Tommy and Jeremy, and that has always bothered Tommy. To him, he has never really lived up to the expectations of Lisa's ex-boyfriend. He didn't put too much stock into it. In this situation, however, the ex happens to be in the picture still as a good friend, always putting Tommy in an awkward position.

Later that evening, everyone retired to their impromptu bedrooms set up by Tommy and Lisa. They had a reasonable drive ahead of them tomorrow and wanted to make sure any jet lag and exhaustion was behind them. The house was quiet. Maurice put his earbuds in and listened to some 90s hip-hop to fall asleep to. He loved the slower, rhythmic beats of the early generation rappers. It helped him fall asleep. He would close his eyes and just focus on the beat, and it worked every time. He slowly slipped away to sleep on the couch in the living room.

Meanwhile, down the hall in the spare bedroom, Jeremy and Tiffany shared the room while Janet slept in the art room which overlooked the bay. There was the sound of quiet bickering as Jeremy and Tiffany argued. The two of them tried to be silent as they whisper shouted at one another. Tommy got up from his bed and gently closed the bedroom door completely. He tried to ignore the noises from across the hall. Lisa had no issue drifting off to sleep. Tommy hated that because he always thought she would be able to sleep through the next world war and never know what happened. She could sleep clean through the apocalypse, whereas he may end up with half a night's sleep, constantly jolted awake by the faintest noises.

Day 2

Maurice awoke to the sun shining directly in his eyes. He rolled over to avoid the rays the best he could, but the room was filled with the breaking dawn light. He lay facing the wrong direction. *Obviously*, he thought to himself, as he muttered aloud while adjusting. Nobody else seemed awake as he checked his cell phone for the morning updates on the world. He made his rounds with his news programs and listened to a podcast while he checked his Facebook. He was up before anyone should be considering being awake, and his whole clock was thrown off. Back home, he should be asleep for easily another three to four hours before work. Here it was 6 AM, and he was up bright and early, ready to start his day.

Down the hall, there was no movement. He knew everyone was supposed to get going soon because the plan was to hit the road by 8 and grab some breakfast on the way. The faint smell of coffee began to fill the air. Maurice didn't like coffee, but he did enjoy the fact it would bring him back from the dead at 6 AM with jetlag. He sat up on the couch, rubbing his face trying to get moving for the day. The only thing that moved him off the sofa was first dibs on the shower. He wasn't sure how Tommy's hot water operated and didn't want to risk being last and suffering through a cold shower before two nights of camping.

Maurice finished his shower and got dressed for the day. As he opened the bathroom door, the smell of freshly brewed coffee wafted into his nostrils. Someone else was awake, so at least he had someone to talk to. He made his way back down the hall toward his belongings in the living room. Passing the kitchen, he glanced inside and noticed Lisa looking out of the back-patio window into the rising sun over the bay.

"Yo. Mornin," he said softly, trying not to disturb anyone else just in case he agitated any night owls in the house.

Lisa glanced at him, then slowly returned to look back out the window. Maurice was not sure what the animosity was about, but he could tell she didn't really like him much.

By 8 in the morning, everyone was up and about, showering and getting themselves together for the trip ahead. Tommy went outside to his driveway and ensured his SUV was cleared out to hold the maximum people and bags he could comfortably. He already took it to the car wash to make sure it was clean outside but wanted to make sure any stupid clutter was out of the way. No need for a passenger to work their legs around a toolbox or other bulky junk. The vehicle was clean and ready to roll. He loaded his and Lisa's bags into the trunk space, leaving plenty of room for at least another bag or two. Jeremy offered to be the second wheel, taking his four-door pickup truck.
This helped because he was able to transport the tents and other bulky items, leaving the personal items in Tommy's trunk.

Lisa came out of the front screen door and joined Tommy by the SUV. She threw her arms around him and smiled.

"Thanks for camping, babe. I know you hate it," she said as she kissed him on the lips.

"I hate it because I hate being dusty, dirty, and gross. I also don't see the appeal of digging a hole to shit in, just saying," he teased as he closed the trunk.

The two slowly made their way back inside the house to see what everyone else was working on. Maurice was charging his phone while checking his social media pages. Jeremy and Tiffany were debating on what was more important to pack for the trip. Janet was in the kitchen drinking a coffee, readily awaiting the signal to load up into the cars. She wasn't much of a talker amongst strangers.

Maurice decided to break the silence. He looked up from his phone and noticed everyone seemed ready to go.

"We all waiting on me? Shoot, let's get breakfast and move this cattle herd."

He grabbed for his bag and started for the SUV. Everyone followed Maurice and dragged their belongings to the driveway. Jeremy and Tiffany loaded up the trunk of Tommy's SUV and began situating the tents and other bulk items in the truck bed. Jeremy pulled out a few ratchet straps he had stowed in the back seat and secured the cargo down. He pulled on them to ensure they were tight and jumped right into the driver's seat. Maurice sensed that there was an issue between him and Tiffany. She slowly walked to the passenger door and climbed in. Janet opted to ride in the truck to give her and Maurice more room to move and breathe in the back seats of their respective vehicles.

Following breakfast, the drive to the campground was pleasant. Tommy felt that the separation between him and Jeremy helped a bit with that. Having his buddy Maurice to chat with was nice. The close proximity also helped Maurice feel a bit better about chatting with Lisa to dissolve any tension between them if any. They all barely talked at breakfast. The service was fast, and food arrived quickly, leaving little time for small talk. He took this opportunity to speak up and relieve the tension.

"So, what's up with you?" he directly asked Lisa, getting to the point.

"I'm sorry?" she shifted to look back toward the back seat.

"Yeah. It's been one day. I met you like, yesterday, and we are already beefin. You didn't say two words this morning. Well, maybe you said two words, but that was about it. Just want to get it off my chest. I like you. If my boy likes you, I automatically like you."

Lisa looked at him, stunned. She thought back to see if she gave him any reason to speak to her like this.

Tommy thought about turning the music up but instead dialed it down lower.

"Ok, so what did I miss?" Tommy asked while taking an exit on the interstate.

54

Maurice was silent. Lisa shifted awkwardly in her chair.

"Well? What's up? Either of you, I don't really care who says something. I just don't like this tension in this car. This is a stress-free space, full of good tunes, and air conditioning. Something I won't have in about a half-hour," expressed Tommy.

Lisa sighed and looked over at Tommy.

"I don't know. He's just goofy, and you become a different person around him," she looked back at Maurice. "Look. I barely know you. Maybe I thought you were an ass after you started talking, but I may have jumped the gun on that. I'm sorry."

Maurice shrugged. "It's cool. Sometimes I'm hard to swallow."

"That's what she said!" Tommy yelled out from the front of the SUV. Lisa shook her head.

"That's what I mean."

Tommy reached forward and turned the radio back up, laughing to himself.

In the pickup truck, there was not much conversation happening. Jeremy focused on the road, while Tiffany and Janet played on their cell phones. They checked everything they could as if this was the last time they'd ever see the internet for the rest of their lives. Jeremy followed Tommy to the exit toward the campground, where they planned on staying. It was nice to live so nearby to a national park, and civilization was not too far away. The vehicles drove down several dirt roads, checking in to the park ranger station to get into the park. The drive to the campsite was long and winding, reaching deep into the wilderness.

Tommy stopped the SUV in front of a large clearing. He waved Jeremy on to pull forward to make it easier to unload the tents and equipment. Jeremy crept the truck along slowly, passing Tommy on his right. He pulled the truck to the far side of the clearing, parking between two large trees. Tommy pulled in across the clearing, opposite the pickup. Everyone began to egress from the vehicles, happy to be able to stretch their legs out. Everyone except for Maurice. Tommy looked around and saw everyone was out and about, looking around except for his friend. He looked back into the SUV and saw Maurice passed out asleep in the seat. The early morning and lack of sleep really took a toll on him, not to mention the obvious jet lag he was still dealing with.

Maurice woke up to two erect tents and music playing. He didn't remember falling asleep and was more upset no one bothered to wake him up. He tried to stretch out a bit and exited the vehicle.

"Good morning, Sleeping Beauty!" Tommy yelled while putting the last tent pole into the tent Jeremy and Tiffany would be sleeping in.

He didn't like outdoors, but he was damn good at putting these tents together. Maurice staggered his way over to the camp area. It was much later in the day, as he could see the sun setting a bit already. He guessed he must have been out for at least two or three hours. Good news, he didn't have to do much to set up, he thought to himself.

Tommy began working on setting up the fire pit area. He knew in the back of his mind he had no intention to set a fire, but he had no issue arranging the stones and gathering the firewood. He arranged several large stones he brought along from the hardware store and placed them in a circle the best he could. He knew this should contain most of the fire, but he still had no idea what he was doing. Maurice tapped him on the shoulder. "You need a hand, boy scout?" Tommy shook his head.

"I have no idea what is going on right now. You have a clue how to make this fire go?" Tommy asked, standing up from the fire pit.

"Hell, I think you just grab a bunch of big ass sticks, throw them in a pile, set the fire, and enjoy. Basic really. I hear even a caveman could do it." Tommy was not amused by Maurice's jokes for once.

Tommy and Maurice set off to collect firewood. Back at the camp, Lisa arranged her and Tommy's bags, trying to get everything sorted out for later in the night when they were too tired to figure out unpacking sleeping bags. She laid out both sleeping bags, and a few hygiene necessities were placed in an easy to reach location. She shimmied back out of the tent to join the others. Tommy picked up four-person tents for the two of them, as well as one for Maurice. He knew with Maurice flying, there was no need to try to check a tent in at luggage. Him buying a plane ticket for a visit was a fair exchange for purchasing a tent, sleeping bag and other camping necessities for him. Lisa walked over to Jeremy and Tiffany's tent. They had a much smaller tent designed for two people to sleep close together, side by side. There was much less room to spread out, and it was clear this was already not a good idea. She could hear arguing and bickering from within the tent.

"Everybody ok in there?" Lisa asked, knocking on the tent as she did.

Jeremy thrust out of the tent in a huff.

"Fine. Fine. We're fine," Jeremy said, a tone of frustration in his voice.

He stomped over toward the truck and looked around in the seats for something he must have apparently lost. Lisa knelt to the door to talk to Tiffany.

"You ok, hon?" Lisa asked.

"I don't know why he has to be such a jerk. I'll be fine. I figured this would be a fun trip, but not with that asshole around."

Tiffany crawled out of the tent. Her eyes were red. Clearly, she had been crying. She did her best to hide it.

"Well, if you want to talk, you know I'm always there for you," Lisa said, trying to comfort her friend.

Tiffany smiled back at her, reassured that she at least had the support of her friend.

Janet set up her tent, the furthest from everyone. She had an expensive looking tent, which came with a load of accessories. For starters, she had a tent that came with a floor. Not the plastic tent floor that came standard with just about every pop tent on the market, but an actual hard plastic floor. She also brought along an inflatable mattress. Lisa headed over to her tent to see how things were going. She knocked on the tent door flap and popped her head into the open flap, which was pinned back from the inside.

"You decent?" she called to Janet, announcing herself in case the tent flap knock was inaudible.

"Holy cow, roughing it much?" she asked, looking around at Janet's tent interior.

Inside her tent was a slew of battery-operated LED lights, a floor, the inflatable mattress, as well as several other amenities of the civilized world. Lisa couldn't believe it.

"We're supposed to be one with nature, not bringing everything to nature," she joked.

Janet smiled.

"Yeah, I'm aware. I just don't like the dark much. Let me know if it's too bright over here tonight, and I'll tone down."

Lisa shrugged. She heard some noise from behind her, the sound of sticks breaking. She turned around to notice Maurice and Tommy were breaking down and setting up the fire pit. It was a good thing they were. It was getting close to sunset becoming nightfall.

Tommy was able to use his fire starters to get a nice fire going for the night. Jeremy brought out a cooler of food he filled stuffed with hot dogs, marshmallows, and alcohol. He offered a beer to Tommy. Shocked, he took it. He was under the impression that there were issues between the two and welcomed the nice gesture. He tossed one over to Maurice as well. Everyone had begun drinking and eating the hotdogs by the fire. Gentle music filled the air as they played Lisa's camping playlist she worked so hard to make over the portable speaker set. Laughter filled the air as each exchanged stories of their high school and college days, full of embarrassing tales and adventures. Tommy felt good that everyone was participating, telling their own stories, or in some cases, each other's. Janet removed herself from the conversation and retired back to her tent. She turned all her lights on and began to read a book, listening to her music as she did.

Maurice added a few bits of wood to the fire.

"Yall want to hear a scary story?" asked Maurice.

Tommy looked up from his hot dog.

"Dude. We aren't 12. Let's not?" Maurice leaned forward, closer to the fire.

"Let's," Maurice whispered.

Jeremy shook his head and smiled, partially in agreeance with the idea. He had a few beers, so he was game for a scary story.

"Go for it, guy," Jeremy said, finishing his beer and opening the next.

Maurice shifted himself in the lawn chair he was sitting in.

"Bet. Ok, so I got one y'all probably haven't heard before. I heard this ish is legit and googled up the craziest story on The Internets. Anyone ever hear the story of Bathell? The Grinning Man?"

He looked around at everyone's faces, blank stares upon each.

"Cool, cool. Ok, so let me begin. Bathell was some ancient god, or demon, or something. You know the supernatural type of dudes. Well, he was worshipped as a god anyway. He used to torture people with their worst fears. If you were scared of snakes, he'd put your ass in a room full of snakes until you died. Scared of water? He would drown your ass, but he'd do it slowly, that was his thing."

The group looked intrigued.

"Ok, I'll keep going. So Bathell was this evil dude in life apparently. One day, the people in his city got tired of his tortures and crazy killing and decided to form an angry mob. They all took him down, set him on fire. Real nasty stuff if you ask me. They said he burned for a whole day. I don't know about how much bodies burn, but I think you ain't supposed to burn for more than like five minutes. But anyway, dude burned for like a whole 24 hours. Now fast forward, they cleaned up the pile of Bathell and tossed his ashes into the river. A few nights later, people started going missing. Nobody could figure it out, and the town was scared. You know, old wrath of God biblical level towns was scared of things they didn't understand," Maurice said, pausing to sip his beer.

"So, this town asked some ancient wise men or whatever, after months of killings and people being found dead. They were always found in some crazy way, but there was nothing actually wrong with them physically. Turns out, they were still being killed by Bathell from beyond the grave. The wise men decided that speaking about Bathell caused the deaths to keep happening. It was like a verbal curse, perpetuated by ancient legends and tall tales. Honestly, it was pretty messed up," Maurice finished as he leaned back in his chair.

The group looked at each other.

"So, that's your scary story? Big deal. What a waste of my time," Jeremy said, standing up to retrieve another beer from the cooler.

Maurice looked offended.

"I don't think you understand this story, good sir. This dude will kill you after torturing you with your worst fear. I read about it online a while back, never really told anyone about it, waiting for the right moment. I assumed a campfire story was the right moment," said Maurice, who was visibly defensive over his tale.

Jeremy took a sip from his beer.

"Yeah, well, how about the story of the Goat Man? That's a thing. Or the Blair Witch? We can go on forever about things that people share with each other that don't exist, and they are not even scary. Hell, the movie they made about the witch wasted my time, too." Tommy leaned forward.

"Ok, guys, chill. It was a good story. That's all it was, so stop being a dick, Jeremy."

"Yo, it wasn't a story. I legit looked it up on some historian website. There was a bunch of stuff about it. People died for real. So that should make it scary," Maurice interjected into Tommy's statement.

Jeremy smugly smiled. Maurice didn't like this guy much and could tell Tommy really didn't either. He had his moments, but honestly, he was just a tool, far as he could tell.

Jeremy looked like he was going to say something but paused and reconsidered his wording.

"So. If you just told us the story, this dude is supposed to kill us now? I'll believe it when I see it. If I tell this Bathell character that I'm scared of Rosie O'Donnell, he's going to send an army of Rosie's to torture me and kill me? It's pretty lame, all things considered."

Maurice quickly spoke back to Jeremy. "No, you don't get it. Dude looks into your brain, finds what you're really afraid of, and that's how you go out. Now that you said it, I doubt this dude is real. Probably as real as Bloody Mary and Candyman. They're just stories," Maurice stood up from his lawn chair and headed to his tent. It was late, and he was not in a good mood. He figured going to bed was better than caving in Jeremy's smug little face.

Tommy was worried that Lisa would have regrets about this whole trip, but he didn't want to ask her if she was feeling anything about how things are playing out. Tiffany eventually slipped off to bed as well. Tommy looked across the fire at Jeremy, who had a few more beers than he should have and visibly appeared drunk.

"You know, I have a real problem with you," Jeremy said, directing his words at Tommy.

Lisa stood up.

"Jeremy! Stop it. Go to bed."

She pointed over at the tent Tiffany went into. He didn't budge.

"You don't know how hard it is to see you two together. It should be me."

Tommy felt uncomfortable and knew the alcohol was talking for him, but there was a lot of truth to everything as well.

"No, he has to hear it. I love you, Lisa. Always have," Jeremy demanded as he slurred his words.

Lisa was embarrassed.

"You have Tiffany. We didn't work, Jeremy, so drop it. It's been years! Now go to bed before Tiffany hears you."

Jeremy didn't budge. Tommy got up from the fire and went off to his tent.

Lisa looked at Jeremy with disappointment.

"Thanks for ruining tonight."

Removing herself from the embarrassment, Lisa went into the tent to join Tommy.

Jeremy sat outside by the fire, muttering to himself. He knew he shouldn't have said what he did. He also knew he was too drunk to think rationally because he could swear he saw someone in the woods. He decided against his best judgment to investigate. He slowly got up from the cooler he was sitting on and finished his beer. Gradually, he staggered his way into the wood line. It was quiet, with only the sounds of a few insects and wildlife giving life to the darkness.

"Hello?" he called out, knowing that he really didn't want to hear a response.

There was nothing ahead of him that he could see as he crept further and further from the campground. He stepped forward through a large brush, pushing several large branches out of his way. Once he pushed through the foliage, he walked into a brightly lit area. It took his eyes only seconds to adjust to the light. He noticed he was no longer in the woods but in fact an open area. He recognized the area. It was his college campus grounds.

Jeremy was confused. He wasn't sure if he had drunk too much or not enough. This was impossible. He must have passed out drunk and be dreaming about this situation. He ventured forth, looking around. He remembered the layout. He looked harder and realized he remembered this day. As he walked along the path, he was approached by Lisa. Visibly younger, he knew this must be a dream.

"Hey, Jer. can I talk to you for a second?"

He was having severe deja vu. He was taken by the hand and led over to a seating area, secluded from the crowds.

"I was doing some thinking. I think you're a great guy. I really do. I'm sure you'll make some woman very happy, but-" she paused, looking visibly upset, "but I don't know that this will work out. We are not meant for each other, and I don't feel the connection with you that I should." Jeremy could feel his stomach twist into knots.

Lisa had a tear run down her cheek.

"Why won't you say something? Why do you never stand up for yourself and be a part of the relationship? Why is it me only making the decisions?
Doing all the talking? It's always me! You need to do a lot of growing up." The conversation made a turn. Jeremy could feel the tension, it was thick in the air. His mind raced. His head was spinning and not from the alcohol. He felt that his mind was as clear as it ever had been. He felt this feeling before. This was the day Lisa broke his heart. It was a happy day prior, the weather was perfect, and he had purchased a ring to propose to her this evening. His heart sank into his stomach upon realizing what day this was. Why would he dream this? He turned himself around and realized he had control of the dream. He began to run. He ran far and fast.

He came into a lit clearing. It was the same seating area that Lisa pulled him into. She stood in front of him.

"Hey, Jer. Can I talk to you for a second?"

She said the very same words once again. He sat through the breakup conversation. It was enough to drive him crazy. He began screaming loudly, running through the campus grounds. He wanted to wake up from the dream. He decided to duck into a building on campus, the math building, as he recalled. He ripped the door open and rushed inside. He found himself immediately in the clearing in front of the seating area once again. Lisa grabbed him by the hand and walked him to the benches.

"Hey, Jer. Can I -"

She was interrupted by Jeremy sobbing uncontrollably. He screamed from his core. He wanted this to stop.

Day 3

Jeremy was awoken by Tommy and Maurice, who were screaming in his face to wake him up. He looked around, confused as to what happened. It was daybreak, and most of the camping gear was packed up. Unsure of what happened, he sat up, not speaking a word or answering any questions he was asked. Tommy didn't know what he was doing last night. Last he saw, he was passed out and slumped over the cooler toward the end of Maurice's story. He gave some half-assed rebuttal that the story was crap and drifted off. How did he get so far away from camp?

"Maybe he went to take a leak and passed out," Maurice said, trying to figure out what happened as well.

After cleaning up a bit and changing clothes, Jeremy felt a little more at ease. He was still very unsettled about what he dreamt last night. Maybe hanging out with Lisa and Tommy drudged up some old feelings in his subconscious.

He thought it best not to bring it up to the group.

"You were screaming. We all came running and found you sitting way out here. You sure you're ok?" Tiffany asked, wrapping her arms around Jeremy.

"I'm good. I think."

Jeremy was still shaking. It all felt too real and took him down a memory trip he would have rather not have journeyed on. He felt pretty useless by sleeping through the entire pack up. He also missed out on some hilarity as well, as Tommy apparently fell in a pile of deer droppings. He regretted missing that moment most of all.

The drive back was quiet in Jeremy's truck. No one really spoke about him being found some distance from the camp, nor did he bring up the dream. He was too embarrassed by it, but it also felt all too real. He could still feel Lisa's hand leading him to that spot. He could still smell the air, hear the sounds. He began to drift off into a daydream about what happened last night, replaying the memories in his head.

"JEREMY!" Tiffany yelled.

Jeremy swerved the wheel back onto the road. Somehow, he had drifted off and lost control of the vehicle. Janet looked terrified in the backseat, as she looked up from her phone. She was checking the latest social media updates and things she missed.

Jeremy signaled to Tommy to pull over. They pulled over at the next wide shoulder they found. Jeremy turned the engine off, put on his hazard lights, and rested his head on the steering wheel. Tommy walked up to Jeremy and knocked on the driver's side window. He slowly rolled it down and looked at Tommy.

"You guys ok? What happened back there?" Tommy asked with genuine concern for the group.

"I don't know. I just had a moment. I should be good in a few moments."

Tommy slowly walked back to the SUV and awaited a signal from Jeremy that he was good. Ten minutes or so went by, and he got a wave and honk from Jeremy that it was time to go.

The ride back in the SUV was a different experience. Tommy and Maurice talked about finding Jeremy in the woods screaming and crying for much of the ride. Lisa was mildly concerned that this was an issue. When they found him, he was crying and yelling her name repeatedly. She needed to know what happened last night. It was going to bother her, mostly due to the fact her name was echoing out through the morning mountain air. Tommy pulled into a small diner just a short distance from his home, and Jeremy followed with his truck. Everyone got out and had an early dinner. It was the quietest dinner anyone had ever had; hardly any words were spoken, save for placing orders and gaining the waiter's attention.

Everyone cleared their bill, and the drive to Tommy's house was thankfully not far. When the vehicles parked everyone, stepped out of their car doors, thankful to just be back in civilization.

"I don't mind if you guys need to shower or whatever. Wash off the nature before you head home," Tommy said as he popped the trunk to the SUV.

Maurice pitched in to help download all the tents and larger items from the truck. Jeremy went inside to sit down for a bit. Everyone could tell something was bothering him, but no one dared ask him. Tiffany went inside to the spare bathroom first and started her shower. Tommy took his tents and chairs and worked on where they should go in the garage.

Jeremy sat in the main den, which was equipped with a large stone fireplace and a glass window view of the bay. It overlooked the pool and the deck that they had been on the day or so prior. Lisa walked by toward the kitchen, and he turned his head slightly to look her direction.

"You ok? You don't seem yourself," Lisa said as she set down the cooler she was carrying.

"I don't know. Something with last night. It felt too real. I'd rather not talk about the dream, though. Let's just move on with the day."

Lisa shrugged at Jeremy's statement. She picked up the cooler and continued toward the kitchen. Tiffany came into the room and sat in the chair across from Jeremy. She didn't say anything. She had just come from the shower and changed.

Tiffany looked at Jeremy for a few more moments but finally decided to ask the question.

"So, what happened last night? You were yelling Lisa's name all morning. That's how we found you. Is there something you're not telling me?" Jeremy got defensive.

"No, there is nothing I am not telling you. I told you. I'm over her, and I'm over this conversation!"

He got up from the couch and stormed across the room and down the hall toward the bedrooms. Tiffany was not happy with the way this adventure played out. She saw Tommy and Maurice sitting on the back of Jeremy's truck bed but didn't want to bother them. She decided to get up and wander before seeing if Jeremy wanted to get back home. She headed toward the kitchen area and rounded the corner to the stairwell that led to the basement. Tommy liked vintage video game systems and always had a Super Nintendo hooked up. Maybe that would take her mind off the drama.

She descended the flight of stairs leading to the basement. It was very nice, with a game room and man cave feel. She went over to the television to turn it on and noticed, there in the reflection, a figure. Something was moving around the corner; she could see it on the screen. She moved quickly, trying to see who was in the basement with her. Around the other side near the bar that Tommy built, she saw a figure, rather, two figures. She moved in closer to get a better look. She saw what appeared to be Jeremy and to her disbelief, Lisa. They were making out in the dark corner of the bar. Her heart sank.

She had been depressed about the fact that Jeremy always compared her to Lisa and that she never felt like she could compete. She knew to see them together, there was no going back. She had nothing left. She felt cold and empty inside.

She tried to turn and run back up the stairs. As she turned, she noticed on the couch, Jeremy and Lisa's nude bodies on the couch, wrapped up in on another in passionate lovemaking. Her mind was racing. She swore they were in the corner, making out just a moment ago. Her emotions got the best of her, and she cried. She cried hard and long. She tried to run back out. Her best attempts futile as her tears filled her eyes, obfuscating the path to the stairs. She just wanted to be out of the room. The sounds of their lovemaking were deafening. Her ears were full of only the sound. She battled with the thoughts in her brain for so long. This was all too much. She wiped more tears from her eyes and tried to gather herself.

Her vision began to clear, and she made her way up the stairs. She didn't pay attention to any of her surroundings. She burst through the front door to the outside. She ripped open Jeremy's truck door and jumped inside. She was still unable to see clearly. Her vision was still blurry, full of teardrops that raced down her cheeks at the frequency of a waterfall. She felt around for the spare key that he kept in the glove box and jammed it into the ignition, starting the engine. She looked up and saw Jeremy walking toward the vehicle, with Lisa not far behind. She threw the vehicle into drive and pressed her foot hard on the gas. The vehicle collided with Jeremy with a loud, audible thud. The crunch could be heard from every room of the house.

Tommy rushed over with Maurice to the driver's side. He ripped the door open and pulled Tiffany out of the seat. Maurice reached in, placed the transmission in park, and turned off the engine. He went to check on Jeremy. He was not moving. Blood covered the front of the truck and the driveway. Tiffany sobbed while being held back by Tommy. Janet came outside, wondering what the commotion was and saw Jeremy. She screamed at the top of her lungs and fainted immediately into the garden near the pavement.

Lisa grabbed Tiffany by the shirt.

"What the hell is wrong with you, crazy bitch!?"

She was visibly shaken by what just happened. Maurice dialed 911.

"He's still breathing. I don't know how this works. I'm not a doctor."

He walked out of sight and spoke with the operator. Tommy let the restraint go on Tiffany and pushed her toward the garage.

"What just happened? What did I miss?"

Tiffany worked to calm her crying down, to get out an audible explanation. Janet came to and joined the group. Tommy offered water to Tiffany from the mini-fridge in the garage, and she took a sip before explaining herself.

"I saw...I...I...saw...I saw your girlfriend and Jeremy hooking up in the basement. I can't believe you'd do this, you slut!" she said as she pointed angrily at Lisa.

"What the fuck are you talking about?" Tommy quizzed, getting visibly angry. "Lisa has been with me and Maurice in the garage. Jeremy was out in the living room asleep on the couch up until you came barreling out of the house!"

Maurice walked back around the corner from behind the garage.

"Cops are on the way. An ambulance too. I have no words right now."

Maurice sat down on the concrete floor in the garage, placing his head in his hands.

Tommy paced the floor.

"How the hell could my girlfriend be making out with Jeremy if she was with me this whole time?"

Tiffany shook her head, sniffling occasionally as she tried to calm down from crying.

"I saw them. She was screwing him on the bar. I saw it. I know I did."

Moments later, sirens were heard from down the road as emergency crews roared up the street toward Tommy's house. EMTs rushed over to Jeremy, loaded him onto a stretcher, and lifted him into the ambulance. Two officers came over toward Lisa, and she pointed to Tiffany, who was still sobbing uncontrollably on the ground. They put handcuffs on her and placed her in the back of the police cruiser. One of the officers came back over to the group.

The officer pulled out a pad of paper and a pen and pointed to Tommy to step to the cruiser. Tommy followed.

"So, what exactly happened here?"

Tommy cleared his throat before he spoke.

"Officer, I honestly don't know. I saw the whole thing, but I couldn't tell you exactly what went down. Maurice and I here, we were unloading and cleaning our camping gear. We just came from a night in the woods, a friend camping excursion. She went inside the house, and the other gentleman you loaded into the ambulance also was inside asleep on the couch. Next thing we knew, she came flying out of the house in a rage, he followed shortly after, she hit him with his own truck, and here we are."

The officer finished scrawling down initial notes. He repeated the process for Maurice and Lisa. Lisa was in no state to speak coherently about her friends.

"We are going to obviously need a few of you that saw the incident to come down to the station. He should be going to the hospital, and we can provide you with the details after we get downtown."

"Is he going to be ok?" Lisa asked, her voice cracked due to all the chaos and stress.

"I honestly don't know. Had she have had more space to get speed, maybe not. For now, all I can tell you is we will get you to the hospital as soon as we can," the officer motioned for the second officer to get into the vehicle, "Here is the address. Please arrive in the next hour or two. We need to get statements as soon as possible."

The officer handed a business card over to Tommy, which included the officers' name and the precinct address.

The police cruisers and other emergency vehicles had all cleared, and Tommy and his friends were left in complete silence.

"What the hell is going on? First, Jeremy is screaming in the woods. Now Tiffany is trying to kill him? What did I miss? Y'all keep some strange company," Maurice said.

After the words escaped his lips, his expression changed. His eyes widened, and his jaw dropped a little.

"Shit. Wait. I think I just figured something out," he turned to the group and rested against the SUV hood, "What if, now follow me on this, that story I told was legit. Like, I looked it up on the internet and thought it was cool, but I didn't think it was real. What if that dude is killing us? Or just making us crazy?"

Tommy looked shocked.

"What do you mean? That story was true? How the hell can a story kill us? Listen, those two had issues from the start, and they were bound to snap at any moment," Tommy asserted, knowing the history between everyone well.

Lisa shrugged.

Janet felt anxious.

"I didn't see anything, so you guys go on ahead. I'm going to head home and try to shake this off," she started toward her car. "Call me if you guys all need me."

Janet got into her vehicle, drove down the driveway and out into the street, disappearing over the horizon.

"Honestly, she probably should have stayed. This is some true horror movie shit, splitting up and everything," Maurice said, trying to liven the mood in the worst way.

"Horror movie? Dammit, dude, that thing isn't trying to kill us. It's a story. Stories don't kill; people do. Tiffany must have snapped, and here we are. I'm going to go shower and get ready to go to the station. Anyone else care to join?" Tommy asked, starting toward the house.

"I'll join you, but I really love the hot water," Maurice joked.

"The station, ass."

Maurice smiled. He did his best to lighten up the moment and shake everyone from the jitters they felt after what they just witnessed.

Tommy finished his shower in the main bathroom. It was a nice bathroom with a jacuzzi tub, shower, a double sink for his and hers, and overall had a lot of room. He stepped out of the shower, reaching for his towel on the rack. He had a very nice stand-alone shower that was fully finished with the rain shower features and multiple water jets hitting from every angle. The room felt very foggy. The shower didn't usually steam up a room this way, and he assumed maybe the vent was blocked by something. The shower wasn't even that hot. He disregarded it and stepped toward the sink to brush his teeth to prepare for the questioning he was walking into.

A thought flittered through his mind as he pulled the mirror forward on the medicine cabinet, reaching in for his toothbrush and floss. He reflected on what Maurice said about this being like one of those horror movies, and the thought flitted through his brain in an instant. He was scared to close the medicine cabinet mirror. He decided it was all too crazy and closed the cabinet door. There was nothing. He wiped some of the steam from it and still nothing. He laughed out loud to himself as he brushed his teeth. The whole idea is just absurd. He finished cleaning his teeth and opened the cabinet to put his brush away. The water in the jacuzzi turned on behind him. As he turned to look back, he closed the cabinet door. Nothing stood behind him.

Maybe the water is acting stupid, he thought.

As he looked back to the sink, a figure stood in the empty space by the tub that he just glanced at. It was tall and very dark. The only thing that was very clear was a large, gnarled grin pasted across what should be its face. His heart sank. He knew he must be going crazy because there was no way something or someone was standing in the bathroom with him. He turned his head around slowly. The figure was gone. The tub was still running across the room. He shrugged it off. His heart was still racing. He had no idea what he had just seen, if he even saw anything at all. He started to walk slowly toward the tub, careful to not slip on any water as he did. As he approached the tub, he could see it was full of water. He turned and reached over, shutting off the faucet knobs. Once the water stopped, Tommy slowly reached his hand into the water to pull the drain plug.

As he reached in, he felt a force behind him shove him into the tub. He went into the tub torso first, hitting his head on the porcelain material as he went in. His head hurt. His aching head was the least of his concerns, as he felt something pushing his face into the water. He panicked and thrashed, trying to get away, but to no avail. He gasped for air each time his face surfaced, which became less and less each time. He knew he wouldn't be able to continue much longer as his body was tiring from fighting back against this force, who seemed to have limitless energy. He began to fade out. He could feel he was taking water in with each second. He coughed and choked on the water as it slowly filled his lungs. His world had begun going dark, and it was extremely hard to fight back to push away from the tub any longer. Maurice heard a commotion coming from the bathroom down the hall. He had just finished using the guest bathroom in the basement, which had a shower stall in it. He walked down slowly toward the room.

"You ok? Stop playing with your rubber ducky in the tub so violently," Maurice called down the hall.

The thought also occurred to him that maybe Tommy and Lisa were in the bathroom together, and they were having some private time.

"If yall are getting your freak on, I can go sit on the deck," he yelled out down the hall.

Lisa stepped out of the bedroom.

"Who's getting their freak on?" she asked as she came out of the master bedroom, which had a master bath attached to it.

Maurice's facial expression changed. He stepped faster toward the door and banged on it. He listened, as he could hear splashing and choking. He tried the knob, but it was locked.

"Yo, you got a way in? Keys or something? Tommy is choking, and he doesn't sound ok," Maurice told Lisa.

She shook her head as her eyes widened with concern. Maurice shrugged and used his weight to bust down the door as best as possible. He slammed his body into it several times before the door lock gave. Once he stepped inside, he noticed the room was thick with hot steam. The vent fan was audibly running but was clearly not working. He looked over to his right at the tub. There he saw Tommy lying motionless, his upper body resting under the water of the tub. He rushed over and pulled him out of the water, laying him on the floor.

"Get in here, Lisa!!!" he called out the door.

Lisa was already coming through the door. She screamed.

"Listen, calm down. I took like a half a class of CPR, I'm gonna give it a shot. Call the ambulance."

Maurice started doing chest compressions on his friend. He turned his head to the side, so the water had somewhere to go.

Maurice resorted to mouth to mouth.

"Don't judge me if you come to, and we lock lips, bro."

He began pushing air into Tommy's lungs. Maurice continued to compress Tommy's chest.

"Not this way, bro. Blaze of glory. Not like this. Not naked in your bathroom covered by a small towel. Come back to me dude," Tommy was still not breathing.

Maurice screamed down the hall, "Are they coming? What's the word?"

Lisa popped her head back into the room, visibly shaken and upset. She rushed over to Tommy.

"They're coming. He's not breathing. Is he ok? Will he be ok?"

Lisa was growing more frustrated and upset.

"I'm doing all I can. I work at a copy shop. I'm not a doctor. This is all I got," Maurice snapped back, letting his emotions take over for a moment.

Lisa rushed off to open and unlock the front door for the EMTs to get inside the house. This is the second incident they were responding to at this house, she thought. What will they say about all of this? She brushed off that thought and rushed back to Tommy and Maurice in the bathroom. She came through the door, hoping he would be sitting up and talking. She was, however, greeted by Maurice sitting on the floor next to Tommy. Her heart sank. She felt sick, unable to speak, cry, or even move. She didn't even realize the EMT crew had pushed past her and attended to Tommy. She couldn't believe what was going on. First Jeremy, and now Tommy?

The EMT crew worked a few moments to try to resuscitate Tommy, to no avail. They looked over at Maurice, who was stunned.

74

"You did what you could, sir," the paramedic said to Maurice, trying to console him with commending his efforts.

Lisa didn't want to hear their words. She didn't want to believe it. She went into the hall and sat against the wall. Her breathing was heavy and hard. She felt panicked and trapped, but she was in the large opening of the hallway. Her world was spinning. She just wanted to have Maurice come out and say it was a big prank the two pulled, but she saw the blood on the bathtub. She saw his body.

Tommy was dead. The paramedics called the time of death at 4 PM. Maurice emerged from the bathroom and wrapped his arms around Lisa to do his best to comfort her. Even being almost a stranger, he knew his place and that he needed to be strong for her. He had no words. No "I'm sorry" would ever suffice. He also remembered they had to be at the station to speak to that cop about the other craziness that took place just an hour or two ago. He decided to try to bring that up.

"So, we still have to go to the station. One thing at a time, Lisa. I'll go down there if you want to be alone here for a bit. I'll just pull up directions on my phone and head down if you want."

Lisa did not want to be left alone. She knew deep in her mind and heart; alone is the last thing she wants. If Maurice was offering to drive, she would tag along to take care of the issue with Tiffany at the station. After all, Tiffany was loosely her friend, through Jeremy. She also needed to check-in at the hospital. She composed herself as best as possible and told Maurice she wanted to go and did not want to be alone. The two got into Tommy's SUV, and Maurice took the wheel. He made several adjustments to the seating and mirrors since he was a little bigger than Tommy. Lisa sat quietly in the passenger seat, looking on her phone. Maurice didn't ask what she was looking at. He punched in the directions to the onboard GPS in the SUV and started down the road.

The two pulled up to the station only fifteen minutes later. It wasn't far from where Tommy's home was located. Maurice shut the engine off.

"You ok to do this?" he asked, with concern in his voice.

Lisa nodded. This was all too much to process, and she needed closure on one thing before she could move to the next. She and Tommy had only been together for a few years, but she knew Jeremy for a long time. She wasn't sure who impacted her worse with today's events. Her boyfriend obviously was the top choice, but Jeremy was always a long-term friend. Both of her losses were devastating. She unbuckled her seatbelt and stepped out of the SUV. The two slowly walked toward the police station.

Maurice did most of the talking inside the station. Lisa was fairly shut inside herself, which was understandable. He spoke to the receptionist, who paged in the officer whom they spoke to earlier today. He came out and shook Maurice's hand.

"Detective Stanley. Glad you guys could come out here. Sorry for bringing you out so shortly after the traumatic experience, but we want to ensure we don't lose any pertinent details," He motioned toward the direction of his desk.

The group walked over, and he sat down across from Maurice and Lisa.

"We have your friend, Tiffany, in custody. We will obviously be looking to have charges pressed, based on the initial findings. She admitted to being behind the wheel because she had caught the victim and, I believe," Stanley paused for a moment, clearing his throat, "yourself, miss." "I was in the garage with my...my..." her eyes welled up with tears.

Maurice put his arm around her.

"Bruh. So, a twist of events, her boyfriend hit his head on the tub and drowned," Maurice said as did his best to keep it together and get the information across.

"I'm sorry?" Detective Stanley asked as he leaned forward.

"Yeah. A few moments after you left, we all tried to clean up from camping. I guess he slipped and drowned in the tub. I don't even know why he was taking a bath. He hated standing water," Maurice added.

Lisa looked up from her tears.

"He was severely aquaphobic. He wouldn't go near the pool we owned either. I don't think he was taking a bath. The shower was about as far as he

would go," she struggled to get words out.

She started to cry a bit.

Maurice looked up as if he had an idea or thought pop in, but quickly dismissed it. It was not the time or place to explore crazy theories. Deep in the back of his mind, he really thought there might be something to this story he told. As Lisa sobbed to the detective about details, the circumstances surrounding Tommy's death, Maurice drifted off into his deepest thoughts. What if this story actually had credibility? What if this ancient dude was killing people? He thought to himself and was quite lost in the moment until he heard his name called.

"Maurice!"

He jolted back into reality.

Detective Stanley stared him down.

"I asked you what exactly you saw outside by the garage. I understand everything is tough right now, but I need you to tell me what happened. What exactly happened?"

Maurice took a deep breath and exhaled.

"Ok. It's going to sound crazy. I told this crazy story when we went camping, right? So, apparently, it might be true. This ghost dude from back in the day kills people if you talk about him."

Detective Stanley's expression didn't shift the entire time.

"So, you're saying Bloody Mary or whatever is going to come to get me if we talk about this thing? This is what killed your friends? I don't believe it," His expression softened, "I don't mean to be that guy, but I've seen enough scary movies. I don't want to be the cop at the end of the movie that finds out the hard way you kids are telling the truth. Nor do I want to catch an ax to the back from the serial killer because that is the nastiest way to go. Every time I see that in a movie, I cringe. Give me a chance to take the bad guy head-on, that's what I say. Go down swinging. Sneak attacks are cheap." Maurice seemed puzzled. Was the cop actually hearing him out?

"So, do you want to hear about this dude? Or you just fucking with me, because I can tell you this story if you want," Maurice smiled, eased by the fact the officer who was questioning him was relatable.

"No, another time. What I do want to know is why your friend went nuts and tried to kill her boyfriend also at the same time how your boyfriend tragically passes."

Lisa was still inconsolable, and the direct tone of Officer Stanley didn't help her.

"Listen. I just want to help and get to the bottom of this. If your friend needs help, I'm here to put her on the path to it. If she had ill intent, I need to know."

Maurice leaned forward to answer. Knowing he was of most sound mind and able to articulate a few words, he felt it best for him to answer.

"Look, officer dude, I'm not sure. I barely know these guys, except for Tommy, who, as you know, is no longer with us. I'm pushing past my loss to give you the best details. Best I got is that one chick just snapped because I was with Tommy and Lisa in the garage. She saw Lisa with her man, who truthfully, had been kind of a dick the whole time I've known him. They were bumping uglies or something in the basement. Dude was asleep in the living room. We all saw him when we came inside to put beers in the fridge and grab some water."

Officer Stanley scribbled notes onto his pad.

"Mmmhm. So, would you say she has mental issues?"

Maurice's jaw dropped a bit.

"Look bruh. I don't want to play detective and solve the Scooby-Doo mystery for you, but I told you. The ghost dude, Bathell. It's him. Her. Or it.

I don't know how it liked to be identified, but that's what did this. I know it." Officer Stanley slammed his pen down.

"Listen, I'm not going to write about how Casper The Pissed Off Ghost killed your friends. It doesn't make sense. Me personally? I'd be requesting for that friend of yours Tiffany to be locked away for being a nutjob, but that's just me. I'd drop all of this 'Bathell' business. Nobody kills you just for talking about it. It's a movie plotline and a bad one at best. It's been done." An officer burst into the door.

"Detective. Something has happened over in the holding cell. I think you should take a look at this."

He left the door open and went down the hall. Detective Stanley collected his belongings.

"Ok, I have to handle something. Get your stories straight and collect yourselves. When I come back, we will take a few moments, and then you guys are free to go. Ok?"

Maurice and Lisa both nodded. Lisa blotted tears from her face with the tissue on the table.

Detective Stanley started for the door when someone yelled from down the hall, "She's hung herself! Get the door open now!"

Maurice and Lisa leaped up from their seats and followed Detective Stanley down the hall. He didn't realize he was being followed until he was inches from the open cell door.

"Jesus H. Christ! Don't do that! I hate people sneaking up on me. Get back in the room right now."

Maurice and Lisa didn't budge. Detective Stanley moved in to take a look at what was going on. Tiffany was in her cell. Her shirt was ripped to shreds, and those tattered pieces used to fashion a noose. It was thrown over the light fixture from the ceiling. It was apparent it was already too late as the first officer to move in cut the line down. Detective Stanley moved in to take a better look. She was still handcuffed to the bed. Even with her one arm free, there is no possible way this would work. He had questions.

Lisa peered through to see what had happened. As she did, the officers cleared the way. She noticed the cold, lifeless body of one of her friends lying haphazardly on the bed. She couldn't even get out a scream, a cry, or any emotion. Lisa stood there, shaking, and just felt cold. Maurice, luckily, was able to hold it together. He didn't know the words to say, but he put his arm around Lisa and walked her back to the room they were getting questioned in. He sat her down, closed the door slightly, and sat down next to her. He had no idea what to say, how to say it, or what to do. He had a hamster die once. That's the closest he had ever gotten to death, and he was eight when that happened.

A few moments later, Detective Stanley came through the door, closing it behind him. He sat down and put his head in his hands.

"Fourteen years on the force. I've seen just about everything. I've never really seen something as crazy as what you and your friends are sitting through right now. I need a coffee. You guys need a coffee?"

Maurice shook his head. Lisa didn't look up at all. She sat with her arms crossed, head down, and shut down from the world.

"Ok, I'm going to head out, get a few details about what happened, and I'll be right back."

Maurice looked up.

"Hey, wasn't she handcuffed? How the hell you gonna hang yourself with handcuffs on? I'm telling you, Bathell is out here, killing everyone! I need a computer."

Detective Stanley opened the door and looked back at Maurice. "Ok, we'll talk about all of that soon. Officer Ritchie will be outside the door if you need anything."

Stanley pushed up his sleeves as he left the room.

Detective Stanley walked down the hall to the coffee machine.

"Out of Order. Great," he read the sign aloud that was slapped across it.

He remembered that upstairs, a few doors away from the Chief's office, there was a nice Keurig machine. He could go for one of those flavored coffees. He took the stairs because the elevator moved way too slow for his liking. One flight wasn't going to kill him, he thought. He made his way up the stairs, winding up the staircase toward the second floor. He opened the stairwell door and made his way down the hall. The second floor was empty, as everyone was dealing with the crisis downstairs. He found the machine on a small table inside a nook in between the restroom doors.

Stanley reached in to grab a flavor pack. They had all kinds of fruity crap, but he was a regular coffee drinker. This would take a moment to figure out something semi-normal. They had one called "Donut Shop," and he figured, going against stereotyping, he liked that the best. He popped that one in, stuck a cup under and hit brew. As he did, the lights flickered.

"Damn. Sumbitch uses that much power, huh?" he said out loud to himself.

No one was around to hear it. The machine started to spit water and coffee into the cup. As the water shot down to the bottom of the paper cup, he heard something clang down the hall. It came from towards the Chief's room, or one of those neighboring rooms. He walked down slowly, toward the end of the hall.

"Hello? Everyone ok down there?" he called out, trying to see if anyone needed assistance.

No answer came back. He made his way down to the first door, which was left ajar. He pushed it open and moved in. No one was inside the room, and nothing was in apparent disarray. He moved on to the next office. The door stuck slightly, so he put some weight behind it. That moved it open. Once the door creaked open, he noticed the room had no window. It was very dark, save for the bit of light flooding in from the hallway. He reached for the switch. Nothing happened.

"Oh, that's not ominous or anything. Anyone need help here?"

He heard a shuffle come from behind a row of filing cabinets across the room. He reached for his flashlight and shined the beam, cutting through the dark and dust of the room.

Stanley began to walk cautiously toward the source of the sound. Flashlight at the ready, maybe some wild animal got in or something. He didn't want to go down in history as the officer that lost the fight to the raccoon. He looked around by the cabinets. Nothing was there. As he went to turn around, he saw a figure out of the corner of his eye. A large, shadowy figure towered him in height. He whirled around to see, but nothing was there. He hated it when his eyes played tricks on him. He checked the area behind the partition and the desk, but no animal or anything was to be found.

"Messing around in this damn dark ass room looking for a squirrel. They don't pay me enough for this business," he muttered to himself.

He checked under the desk, but no animal scurried out.

As Detective Stanley stood up, he felt as if someone or something was standing behind him. He went to turn around but felt as if his feet were frozen in place. He moved his head slightly as he felt a sharp, burning pain in his side. He'd only been stabbed once before on the job during a domestic dispute response case, and he was having flashbacks on that pain. He knew what that pain was. The housewife popped out from behind him as he tried to ask the husband what happened. She stabbed him in the back three times. He made it out of there, and it truly helped the husband's case that his wife was crazy. This pain he was currently feeling felt all too familiar.

He was able to turn his head slightly more and see a towering, shadowy figure looming over him. It must have been six and a half feet tall by his measure and stocky as all hell. The only thing he could make out was a large, grinning mouth full of gnarled teeth. He felt the stabbing pain again. This time it was slightly lower, near the kidney area.

"Goddammit, not today, motherfucka!" he yelled out and pulled all his weight from his feet and began moving again.

Stanley ran, feet heavy, down the hall. There was still no one on his floor, and that was odd to him. He looked behind him, and nothing followed. Stanley knew this was not cool, and someone was in the station as a threat. He needed to get downstairs and warn everyone and lock down the building.

He made his way to the stairway exit, pulling open the door as he did. He went through the doorway and made his way to the top of the stairwell. From behind the wall near the door, he felt a presence nearby. He pushed past the entity. He felt a massive force brush past, as well as another stabbing pain in his upper back. He barely acknowledged the blood trail he left from the room to the stairs was pooling up under him at this point. He looked back toward the wall and noticed the crazed housewife, smiling as she did the day she stabbed him. She was holding the kitchen knife in her hand. She was exactly the same as the day he met her, not a detail out of place. He shook off the thought and pushed his body further to descend the stairs.

As he went down the stairs, his feet still felt heavy. He barely felt the energy to cry out for help and attempted a half yelp as he took the first step down the staircase. He felt as if his arms were equally as lethargic and unable to move. He figured his brain was getting the best of him and pushed on. Stabbing sharp pains filled his body as he felt another knife wound piercing through his shoulder blade. He made his way to the bottom of the stairs and went to pull open the staircase door. He noticed his hands were coated in blood as he grabbed for the handle. He stumbled and shambled through the hall, calling for help. For some reason, no one could hear his cries. Stanley grew more frantic as he stumbled forward. His vision blurred. He called for help once more, feeling his way down the hall. He felt a hand touch his shoulder, which he struck out at.

Lisa heard a commotion coming from outside the door.

"Maurice, what is going on out there?"

He shrugged his shoulders and got up to open the door. Once he reached for the door handle, the door swung open. Detective Stanley stood there, dropping to one knee. He was assisted by Officer Ritchie to lower him to the ground while screaming for a medic.

"What happened Detective? Is the perp still in the building?" Ritchie asked, the panic was evident in his voice.

"It….it…I…I don't know…" Detective Stanley said, fighting for the energy to speak.

Blood pooled under him. Lisa screamed from across the room.

"Holy shit!" Maurice said as he backed up to give room to the paramedics arriving.

Ritchie told a passing officer that the detective had been attacked, and the perp may still be on the grounds.

"Kid…," He looked at Maurice, who gave his attention to the officer on the ground. "I….be…lieve you. It's rea..-" he slipped off before he could finish, but Maurice knew that this was the work of his stupid story.

He gave enough details that it endangered the cop.

An officer came in and moved Lisa and Maurice to a waiting area. The officers ultimately allowed them to leave, as they really had nothing to go on at this point. Lisa wanted to visit Jeremy at the hospital. He was in the ICU, but she wanted to see the last glimmer of her old life that existed, even just for a moment. It was late in the day, and Maurice wasn't sure what the visiting hours were. He opted to drive to the hospital anyway. The drive was quiet, mostly filled with Lisa sobbing or fighting back her tears. Maurice just sat quietly in his thoughts. This was all too much. He barely knew Lisa or these people, but he felt he had an obligation. He debated changing his plane ticket tomorrow to stick around but knew he had to get back to his girl in Texas.

He pulled into the parking garage for the hospital and helped Lisa to the information desk inside. Jeremy was in ICU, so they gave directions on how to get there as well as where to find his room. They walked down the nurse's station in the ICU, and they pointed to a room across from the desk.

"You going to be ok?" Maurice asked Lisa.

She nodded, and the two went inside the curtain covered room. Inside on the bed was Jeremy. He was scarred upon the face, and most of his body was in a cast. Tiffany had broken bones and body parts that should have honestly killed him. Lisa crept closer, while Maurice held back by the entryway.

"Hey, Jer? Are you ok?" she called out, placing a hand on his hand even though it was fully covered in a cast.

He didn't answer. He was unconscious and was heavily medicated. She sat down in the chair next to the bed. Maurice stepped out of the room to the nurse's station.

"Visiting hours are only for a little bit longer, ok, hon?" the nurse told Maurice.

He gave a dorky double thumbs-up, a smile, and leaned back against the counter. He was still trying to process everything that happened, as well as the loss of his best friend, Tommy.

Jeremy was unconscious since the accident. In his comatose state, he was forced to relive the break up between him and Lisa repeatedly. He had no idea he was in an accident, or that his body was in such bad shape. The only thing he knew was a crisp, autumn air, a gentle breeze, and a devastating breakup. Repeating over and over. He heard in the faint distance a familiar voice but could do nothing. Lisa approached him over and over, leading him to that area by hand, and splitting the relationship. It was killing him. He hated losing Lisa, and the fact he dreamed the same scenario incessantly destroyed him inside.

"Jer, I know you can hear me. They always say you can. I want you to know I'm here for you. I'll always be here for you. I lost Tommy. I've seen so much devastation today, but I know you were always there for me in the past. I can't even have that. I want to be here for you, but I feel I can't even give you my best. Tiffany is dead. She couldn't live with what she did to you, I guess.
When you come out, I'll be here for you."

The heart monitor beeped twice. She looked over at it, as it suddenly began jumping. Jeremy began seizing in the bed. His monitors were screaming and going all over the place.

Maurice sat out by the nurse's station and saw two nurses rush into Jeremy's room. He knew this wasn't good. He was checking his phone for info on Bathell and was coming up with no more information than he already had. There was nothing about people surviving the curse, people making a deal, barter, or anything. So, if this thing was real, there was no way to break the cycle. That didn't help matters any. Doctors rushed past Maurice into Jeremy's room, and Lisa was pushed out. Maurice walked over to her.

"You ok? What happened?"

She couldn't answer. She was visibly distraught and in no shape to answer. One of the doctors came out of the room and met with Lisa and Maurice. His expression said it all. Maurice decided to step forward and ask what happened. The doctor pulled him to the side and spoke to him.

"Your friend here, he was stable. We were treating him for his wounds, but it seems as if he just 'gave up.' It's a shame, really."

He patted Maurice on the shoulder and headed back down the hall. Maurice knew there had to be something to this whole curse thing. If he was doing fine, why would he just die? How does Tommy have a bathtub full of water and drown? How does that crazy chick run her man over after thinking he was cheating on her? It must be true, but it could be that these people are just crazy. Who even knows at this point, maybe he is just drawing conclusions that aren't even there? The thoughts raced through his head.

Maurice offered dinner for Lisa. She needed to get out and shouldn't be alone either. They went to a local 24/7 diner and ate. Appetites were not at their best because even Maurice barely ate what he ordered. No one spoke about everything that happened today. It has just been hectic, traumatizing, and all-around a disaster, especially for Lisa. She had lost her best friend and his girlfriend who was also her friend, as well as her boyfriend. She hadn't even had enough time to process the number of deaths as they happened so frequently and quickly. All of it sat in her chest like a large lump.

After dinner, they traveled back to Lisa and Tommy's home. It was surreal to walk into the house after everything that had happened. There was broken glass on the driveway. A few pieces of Jeremy's truck were strewn haphazardly around from the accident. When they went inside, Maurice knew she was not to see the bathroom. He set her up in the living room, turned on the TV, and went to work to clean the bathroom up. After he scrubbed the blood out of the tub and floor, he returned to see she had passed out from exhaustion. He felt that was a good idea as well and made his way to the recliner across from her and followed suit. The sounds of the tv on low volume, coupled with the faint soothing blue glow it gave, lulled him to sleep almost instantly.

Day 4

The next morning, the sun crept into the living room as it always did. The light flooded the room as the sunrise came over the bay. Maurice was happy to see this because it meant he made it through the night. He looked over, and Lisa was still passed out on the couch. She was snoring loudly, so he knew she made it also. He sat forward on the recliner, stretching his neck and arms, and stood up. The noise of the recliner woke Lisa as she looked at Maurice and smiled. She must have run the same thought process, assessing the fact everyone was alive. The morning felt a little better.

Maurice went over to the couch and sat next to Lisa.

"I have to fly out today. It sucks, but it's whatever," Maurice said, looking remorseful that he had to leave her alone with all of this.

Lisa looked up, her expression shifting as an idea plastered into her mind.

"Janet! I have to call Janet!"

She immediately went over to her phone on the coffee table and dialed up the number for Janet. The phone answered after two rings. "Hello?"

"Hey! Janet!? Is that you? You're ok?" Lisa asked.

There was an awkward pause on the other end.

"Yeah, of course, I'm ok. Why? Are you guys not ok? Was it another bad dream or something? What's up?"

Lisa paused, then took a deep breath.

"Tommy, Jeremy, and Tiffany are all dead." She waited for the response from the silent phone.

Janet worked up the nerve to say or ask anything.

"What? When? Are you ok?"

Lisa composed herself. Saying the words out loud didn't make the situation any more real to her.

"Yes. We are fine, Maurice and I are here. Would there be a way Maurice can bring me to your place, and I stay with you until we sort all of this out?

He flies out today, and I don't want to be alone in this house."

Janet agreed immediately and offered to set up a room for her. The two ended the phone call, and Lisa looked a little more relieved that everything was over.

"It didn't get her, whatever this thing was. So, I don't think your theory works, Maurice. This just had to be a series of flukes. Really unlucky and poorly timed incidents," said Lisa as she went off to pack.

Maurice thought long and hard while he put his belongings together to fly back home. It just didn't add up. Nothing sat right with him. There was no way this was over. It was supposed to be a three-day ordeal, but hey, who's keeping time, really? According to everything he read on any website, lore, or blog, it seemed like the oppression went on for 72 hours. They all should be in the clear, considering that other girl was ok. Lisa joined him in the living room a few moments later, with a small suitcase of belongings.

The two loaded up the small two-door coupe just around the side of the garage. This was Lisa's car, and for obvious reasons, they didn't take it camping. Maurice packed the trunk and climbed into the driver's seat. Lisa locked up the house and went to the passenger side of the car, and the vehicle started down the road after Maurice adjusted the seating from a small 140-pound woman to a 270-pound man. The radio was off, which made the situation more awkward. Maurice reached for the knob.

"May I?" he motioned toward Lisa and turned the radio on low. As they left the neighborhood, Lisa gave directions to Janet's home which wasn't too far from her house.

A feeling crept over Maurice as a thought flashed across his eyes.

"She wasn't there!" he exclaimed while hitting the steering wheel.

Lisa was startled.

"What? Who? What did I miss?"

"She wasn't there! Sonofabitch! She wasn't there! She went to bed early! Remember?"

Lisa sat back and thought about what Maurice said, and yes, she did remember Janet going to bed early. Maybe she didn't hear the story, and she was in the clear this whole time! No wonder she had no idea what anyone was going on about. Maurice rolled the window down and allowed the cool summer morning breeze into the car. It was a delicate balance of warm and cool that made the moment feel just right.

They slowly turned onto the highway and headed down the direction of Janet's home. Not many words were spoken during the drive. They just enjoyed the summer air, the tunes on the radio, and the fact they had gotten through this thing.

"Seventy-two hours, by the way. We made it. I looked it up. This thing sticks around for three days, and after that, I guess you're cool," Maurice said, drumming on the steering wheel to the song on the radio.

Lisa nodded, and a slight smile crept across her face as she turned to look out the window.

"It's this street here. Hang a right."

Maurice turned the vehicle down the road.

The car stopped in front of a nice Cape Cod style home. The yard was nicely decorated, and it was clear Janet liked to garden. She was standing on her front porch, as Lisa leaped out of the car and ran towards her. They embraced, and Maurice could hear Lisa say, "I'll tell you what happened to everyone when I'm ready." He parked the car, grabbed their bags, and headed toward the house. Maurice dropped his bag by the front door and carried Lisa's into the living room area. He joined Lisa and Janet in the dining room as they sat down for a coffee.

"Maurice, coffee?"

He shrugged and accepted a cup. He sat down and joined the ladies at the table.

"Hey, my flight is in a few hours. I know yall's TSA is crazy, so I'm going to head out in a bit. I'll grab a cab. Don't worry about driving me. You do you. Oh, here's my number if you need anything."

He held his phone up with his phone number plastered on it. Lisa, as well as Janet, entered it into their phones.

After about a half-hour or so of the ladies conversing, Maurice felt the opportunity to step away and head back home. He finished his coffee, took it to the sink himself, and excused himself from the room to call a cab to the airport. He came back into the room after a few moments and said his farewells, and started for the front porch to await the cab. He sat down on the porch swing out front, taking in the scenery and the quietness of everything.

Lisa came out onto the porch a few moments later and joined him.

"Thanks for everything. I mean it. Tommy would have been glad to know how good of a friend you are. I'm glad you are, or were, his friend."

Maurice smiled.

"I still am his friend. Don't get it twisted. He owed me twenty bucks. He ain't getting out of it this easily. He just has to wait a while to pay me up."

Lisa laughed slightly at his bad joke and pointed to the cab creeping down the road.

"That's you, I guess."

The two exchanged a hug, and Maurice walked down the stairs toward the cab.

"I'll call you or text you when I land, cool?"

Lisa nodded and waved to him as he got into the cab and watched him disappear around the corner. She slowly turned and went back inside the home to join Janet in the living room, who had turned the television on to have some background noise. Lisa walked past Janet and went to the bedroom she had set up. She threw herself onto the bed and cried long and hard. In all her life, she couldn't remember a time when she just wanted to do nothing but cry for hours on end. She hadn't had a moment to really process what had all happened, and it finally caught up to her.

Tommy, Jeremy, and Tiffany. Even that cop, she saw die right in front of her. Everyone. It was all too tragic. Janet could hear her but didn't want to interrupt. She felt it best to wait it out until she was calmer. It sounded like she needed this.

Maurice arrived at the airport with no issues. He sat through the TSA for almost an hour and got to his terminal. He had no delays or issues, and he was just happy to be on stage one of the journey back home. He looked around for a stupid gift or some kind of souvenir he could bring his girlfriend since she couldn't make the trip. He wanted to call her and tell her he was on his way, but she was at work. He figured a text before wheels up would work just fine. He meandered through the airport, looking at all the different shops. He even stopped for a cinnamon bun before heading to his terminal for boarding.

Once at his terminal, he sat down and sighed a deep breath of relief. He put his headphones in and listened to his music. The music drowned out just about everything hustling and bustling around him. The flight attendant called his boarding numbers, and he saw the screen flip to BOARDING for his flight. He packed his electronics up and began the boarding process for the plane. This was a big step toward getting back home, and he could hardly contain his excitement. He had a nice window seat because he liked to lay his head against the wall and pass out asleep. The trip from Maryland to Texas was a long one, and he managed to grab a flight without any layovers. It was the unicorn of flights as far as he was concerned.

He set up shop in his seat. He placed his tablet and headphones in the pouch in front of him, ready to watch a movie if he couldn't sleep. He hated flying, and the last thing he wanted to do was be aware of the fact he was on a plane. He already took pills for motion sickness and was ready to order as much alcohol as it took to forget flying. He adjusted himself into the best-relaxed position and braced for takeoff. This was the part that scared him the most. It wasn't the in-flight; after a while, it feels like being in a car or a bus. The takeoff and the landing are the two that feel the worst.

As the plane began to taxi to the runway, passengers were greeted by the flight attendants. They went through the routine motion of the normal safety course prior to takeoff. Maurice made sure his window was closed and paid no attention if anyone else had one open. As long as he could focus on something other than flying, he was in business. Moments later, the plane was prepared for departure and ripped off toward the sky in a successful takeoff. He kept his eyes closed and did his best to ignore life around him until the plane leveled.

"How the hell do people do this for work all the time?" he thought to himself, as the plane continued its climb to its appropriate altitude.

After a few minutes, which felt like hours to Maurice, the plane leveled out, and everyone was permitted to pull out their devices. Attendants came by with carts full of snacks, sodas, and booze. He opted for the booze, trying to calm his nerves. He quickly finished the bourbon he ordered and put in for a second round before pulling out his tablet to watch some television shows. He figured watching some Game of Thrones should tie up plenty of time. He had to catch up and see if the dragons ever came. He began the first episode and made himself as comfortable as he could in his corner, propping up the show on the tray table in front of him. Winter hadn't even come, nor had Sean Bean been killed before Maurice found himself asleep.

Maurice was jolted awake by a large amount of turbulence. The plane was bouncing quite a bit, and the fasten seatbelt signs were glowing. He had his seatbelt on by default. He didn't trust planes and didn't want to risk it. He looked around and saw no one was panicking, so there must have been no reason to worry. Against his best judgment, he lifted his window up a bit to see how the weather was outside. It was clear, and he could see into the horizon. Except there was one problem: the horizon was facing the wrong way. The plane was falling. He looked back into the cabin, and not a soul seemed worried. How could they not be worried?

He unbuckled his seat belt and leaped over the guy next to him into the aisle.

"Sir, can you please sit down?"

The flight attendant asked him as she met him in the aisle. Maurice was even more panicked by the fact that she wasn't even mildly worried about what was going on outside. He pointed to the window.

"We are crashing bitch! Don't you see? How are you so calm?"

He gripped onto the chairs as hard as he could to keep from falling in the plane.

"I don't know what you're talking about, sir. Now I will ask you again to refrain from using foul language toward me. Calm down, and please take your seat."

The plane bounced hard another time.

"Hell naw, give me a life jacket and a parachute. I want off, and I want to live."

Two more attendants came up to him.

"Sir. Last time. Please sit down!"

The larger male attendant put a hand on his shoulder. Maurice didn't want any trouble. Something was clearly wrong here. He sat back down.

He buckled his belt back around himself and looked out the window. Everything was fine. The scenery was the right direction. There was no smoke, fire, or anything worth causing alarm over, save for a bit of bump in the air of turbulence.

"Jesus. Am I losing it?" he thought to himself.

He put his tablet back on and tried to resume watching the show. This time he felt he would not have the ability to fall asleep. He intently focused on the show, trying to shut out the world around him once again. He would glance out the window periodically, verifying the world was the right way up.

Another episode or two passed, and the announcement came over the intercom that they were a half-hour out from the airport. Maurice was happy about that because it meant being back on the ground and getting back to normal. Especially with being in the air and his little freak-out moment, he was relieved he was nearing the end of this chaotic madness people call flying. The pilot began spouting off the weather, local time, as well as a few other details regarding the landing patterns, but Maurice didn't care. He continued to focus on his episode after he closed his window. He was almost home free, and he was relieved.

By the time the plane began its descent, it was already late in the day local time. His devices hadn't updated yet as they were still running airplane mode. The pilot had mentioned the local time was around 6 PM. Given the fact it's a straight shot for almost four hours and the time zone difference, it was not half bad. It was still daylight out, and he was happy about that. The plane grounded only a few moments later. After a successful landing, the aircraft began to taxi to the terminal gate. Maurice flipped his devices out of airplane mode, and the signal started to connect. Text messages and voicemails began to populate on his phone, but at such a large frequency it made it hard to start checking.

Maurice watched as his phone filled up with texts, voicemails, and notifications to the point the phone displayed 10+ to indicate he received a lot of messages. After about a minute, everything stopped. It appeared he got everything that was sent to him at this point. He checked the messages first. Two were from his girlfriend, who asked about his landing time and if he took off ok. He responded to those and moved onto the others. Several

were from Janet. He started reading the messages.

"Pick up the phone! Did you land!? When is your layover, please!"

"Txt me when u get this!"

"Hello? Maurice? Please call or text me bak."

"Call me asap!"

He looked at this onslaught of texts from Janet. What the hell was going on? He wanted to get into the terminal before getting into a call, so he started checking the voicemails. The first one was from Lisa.

"Maurice?! Please answer the phone! That thing isn't done! I'm freaking out and seeing some bad things. It's not looking good, and I need to talk to you. I can't talk to Janet. Please W-!"

The message cut off at the end. The next three or four messages were clearly from Janet. He assumed they were in the same vein as the texts. He clicked the first one.

"Maurice, it's Janet. Something is wrong with Lisa. She's locked herself in the bathroom and has been in there for the past two hours. I don't know

what to do for her. Call me?"

The first message didn't seem as panicked as the texts, so they must have come after.

He listened to the next two messages, one being from his girlfriend and the next one from Lisa. Lisa was panicked once again. She was crying uncontrollably and didn't sound like she was doing too good. She didn't really say much, but the message went on for almost three minutes. He listened to it all. She cried. She apologized. She cried more. As Maurice was leaving the terminal, he sat down to listen to the message again. She apologized for not being stronger, for not being a better friend and a better person. She wasn't apologizing to Maurice. She made it clear, she was apologizing to Janet. The message ended.

The last message was Janet once again.

"Maurice. It's, well, it's me. Janet. I'm here with paramedics. I think the officers want to speak to you since you were involved with everything in the last few days. I don't know too much, but they asked me about something with the police station as well? I gave them your number. They should be in touch. Anyway, Lisa is dead."

There was a strong, silent pause and a huge, shaking breath from Janet over the phone. Her breath into the phone caused the sound to distort for a moment.

"She cut her wrists in my bathtub, Maurice. She cut her wrists. I know she was so happy, and everything changed in the last few days. She hated the sight of blood. She even freaked out about a papercut. It doesn't make sense. She would never get close to a blade if there were a chance she would cut herself."

Maurice was silent. He didn't even listen to the rest of the message. His hand dropped to his legs.

"Jesus," he mumbled out loud to himself.

He checked the time on his phone and began to do some math.

"Wait. So, if I was up in the woods with this story at like 7 or 8 and it's almost 7 now, it must be exact? Damn."

He also thought to himself that he still survived. Does that mean he beat this thing? He had questions. He decided it best to text his girlfriend to head to the airport, or if she's already here, let him know. He began to look up this thing more. There had to be something he missed.

Looking on his pages he had bookmarked, nothing detailed anything involving survivors at all. His math had already been wrong on the amount of time to survive, so what else was he wrong about? He decided to do another search for this curse. In his travels, he found a blog from someone who detailed their whole experience, logging what happened with friends, family, and anyone who came in contact. This was almost the exact same thing that happened to him and the camping group. He continued to read to the end. He was looking for any detail, anything that could be overlooked, or a minor detail of any sort.

The last log for the weblog by this guy reads like what Maurice experienced. The author had a moment where he thought this would be his last, but he kept his wits about him. Had he have been alone, he would have been a goner. Luckily, the people at the local coffee shop he was writing this pulled him back into reality. He realized that being alone is key. He continued to read.

"You have to be alone and isolated for this thing to really do a number on you. Even so much as a different room than everyone else. So much as a partition in between you. In the office at a different cubicle.

Anything. Isolation does it. I think that's the key to beating the odds. I only wish I knew sooner."

Maurice sat back on the bench he was sitting on trying to process everything. It's true. Looking back, even though Tiffany was in front of everyone when she ran the dude over with the car, she was alone at some point in the house. He thought even more. Tommy was alone in the bathroom, and so was Lisa.

He even remembered the police station fiasco. That cop went off by himself, and he heard the whole story. Tiffany got hung while in her cell alone. It all makes sense in a sick way. Maurice felt a little relieved but also sick to his stomach, knowing that he brought all of this into his world.

He received a text that came up from his girlfriend saying she was outside at the pickup. Maurice quietly walked toward the pickup area. He collected his baggage and made his way outside. He calmly walked to the car in which his girlfriend drove. In her excitement, she ran up to Maurice and wrapped her arms around him for a hug. He could barely find the emotion to be joyful.

Everything that happened just weighed down on him like a ton of bricks. She reared back from him and asked, "What's wrong, baby?"

He shrugged and tossed his bags into the open trunk.

"I'd rather not talk about it. Not right now. Maybe one day, but not today." She stopped him.

"No, you're not letting me off that easy. What's eating you?"

He climbed into the passenger side of the car.

His girlfriend got into the driver's seat and began to drive away from the airport. The windows were down slightly, allowing the warm Texas air to flow into the car. He missed this. The woods were nice, but there was something about this state that felt different. His girlfriend pressed harder.

"So, what? You're not going to tell me?"

Maurice closed his eyes for a moment and collected himself.

"So, Tommy is dead. So are a lot of his friends. I may have to fly back for a court date or something. I don't know. I'll find out more later. That's all I'm telling you."

She pulled the car over.

"What did you do?"

Maurice turned to her and said, "I got to talk to this girl Janet up there and find out what she says. Once she tells me what's going on, I'll let you know what I know. All I know is a lot of people are dead, and it might be my fault." She shifted in the seat to look at Maurice.

"Look, baby, tell me what is going on. We don't keep secrets. Tell me everything!"

Maurice looked at her and poured out the whole story. How they went camping and when they returned how Tiffany killed Jeremy. Tommy died in a freak accident; Lisa and Tiffany too. He only left out one minor detail: the fact he knew exactly what was killing them.

"So, who's this Janet? Is she pretty?"

She got more visibly upset. Maurice did not want to even go into details about this, but he was in hot water. He didn't want to lose this girl and was afraid to really discuss it, but he felt being honest was the best thing he could do.

"Ok, I'm gonna level with you. Tommy was dating Lisa. Tiffany was with Jeremy. Janet was the chick that Lisa stayed with when I left after this whole thing went down. We kept in touch only for the sake of if anything happened or if anything changed. There ain't nothing there, so it's cool."

Maurice did his best to be as truthful and forward as he could.

She began to drive again. Her driving became a bit more aggressive, and he could tell she was not happy with him.

"I don't like secrets. I especially don't like my man talking to other women without me knowing. What did she say to you? What was the message?"

Maurice considered holding his phone up to her to read but felt that it was a bad idea. He read it off to her and paraphrased the voicemail. She was visibly more and more aggravated as he talked. He had no idea why in the world she would be getting mad over this. He started to panic a bit.

"I don't know how you're just gonna come up on in my car after being up with some chick in Maryland," she began, "talking about 'you don't know nothing about nothing' and look me dead in my eye sockets like I don't know what the fuck's going on? Like I'm dumb? I ain't dumb. I know what you are doing, Maurice!"

Maurice glanced at the speedometer, which read 88Mph. She was speeding fast.

"You wanna slow down, baby?"

She didn't answer. She just kept muttering to herself, and he could make out only a few words here and there. None of it was good. He looked back at his phone.

He got a text from Janet only a second ago, which he missed in all the confusion. He tried his best to check it out as the car wove in and out of traffic, even running a red light. He was panicked. He didn't know she was this crazy, and they'd been dating for a few years now. He thought this was the game changer with her. His last ex risked his life too many times, and it frankly scared him to death. That girl had a death wish and put his name on the list with her, and this felt all the same in the car. He read the text.

"I don't think I'll be able to sleep right. Last time I had a hard time sleeping, you guys were whooping and hollering outside my tent, and I had to turn my headphones up. I know it wasn't even 7:30 when I passed out. Call me when you can. I'll be up probably."

He looked at the clock. It was an hour difference, so his clock read 6:26. He did some mental calculations. As he tried to figure things out, his girlfriend

was not having it from the look on her face.

"Oh, is that this bitch on the phone right now? Tell her I said hello!" she screamed as she ran a red light.

Maurice even weighed the option of tucking and rolling, but at this speed, he had a better chance of surviving a crash. His girlfriend continued to have her foot on the gas. He decided one last-ditch effort.

"Baby, I love you. You're my world. Please stop! Don't do something crazy you'll regret!"

She didn't look over. She didn't budge. A minute went by, which felt like an eternity to Maurice. Suddenly she slowed the car, and it went back to a reasonable 35MPH for the area. She rolled the windows down all the way.

"So, where you wanna eat baby?" she looked over and smiled.

Maurice was confused, terrified, and perplexed as to what just happened. Now that the car slowed, he was able to figure it out. He dreamt about the airplane issues. That was all a bad dream because no one said a word to him for the rest of the flight. His real fear? Crazy women. It dawned on him.

He took a moment to understand why it stopped and realized that this was the exact moment he told the story, 72 hours ago. He managed to make it out of all of this and was 100% in the clear, based on what he knew.

"Well, where you wanna eat? Otherwise, I'm picking somewhere you don't like," his girlfriend said jokingly.

"Damn, Traci. I don't know, but I could use some breakfast food."

She punched in directions to the nearest diner that served breakfast food. The two got out and ate, and Maurice worked as hard as possible to act like the last 20 minutes didn't happen. He felt it best to keep that to himself, to bury that along with the story he found on the internet that changed his life forever. As he drank his coffee, the burden he felt the past three days was gone, and he knew he had to hit the internet hard to work to pull this story down and write a how-to guide or something. Maurice had work to do.

The End

Some Notes On Bathell

I originally started this ordeal out way back in the wee years of 2013. I wanted to make a movie. I threw down a script of your typical teen slasher with a supernatural twist, but as I grew older, I looked back at this script more and more and felt that it always needed more. I also couldn't sucker anyone into acting in a movie written by a guy who never so much as filmed anything outside of a web series before.

I was always passionate about this idea, though. The idea of this spooky ghost dude and the way he killed. I decided it was best to throw away my original idea of ten teenagers in the woods and mature the story a bit. What you read today is the story I jazzed up from my movie script. A lot of the people are based on me or a few friends, using their thoughts, relationships, and fears as fuel for the story.

I did my best with trying to make some characters that everyone could connect to and steering from the obvious setups that could be predicted. Thanks to several friends and other people, I was able to base characters around individuals I knew or gained insight into how police interact. I was able to tweak and spin a few things to make what I think is my favorite story. The unfortunate thing, I started writing this years ago, only to be beaten to the punch years later by films like the Bye Bye Man. Granted, my dude doesn't have a silly name, but it's a similar psychological ride.

I hope everyone digs it since it's my first foray into horror. I feel it's good and want to make more scary stories. I grew up on Scary Stories to Read In The Dark and classic horror movies. I always found supernatural and unexplained things fascinating. Killing a baddie like a Michael Myers or Jason was always fun for me, but they didn't have the same sway as demons, ghosts, and the supernatural killers, especially like Freddy. Maybe you guys will feel for these characters and all the things I put into this book! Thanks for reading!

-Harry

About the Author

Harry Carpenter was born in Baltimore, Maryland. He enjoys cosplay, music, and horror movies. As a young author, he took a stab at writing science fiction stories. Now, he is working to build a science fiction universe in a novel, as well as tell life stories and real horror experiences.

He is a cat lover as well.

Twitter: @FuzzyWoodworker
www.facebook.com/hcarpenterwriter
www.hcarpenterwriter.com

Also by Harry Carpenter

Tales From An Ex-Husband: 2019
Brain Dump (Poetry): 2019

FUBAR: Blackout: 2020
Memoirs of a Crazed Mind: 2020

Made in the USA
Monee, IL
05 February 2021

59699846R00066